For my wife Renee:

My muse
My confidence
My heart

Grim Fate

Published by Reading Nook Publishing

Published 2024
First edition published 2020, Second edition published 2020, Third edition published 2023.

ISBN: 979-8-9878657-2-9

GRIM FATE

CHAPTER 1

The autumn leaves slowly tumbled to the ground in a graceful dance that reminded the man of a dream he had once upon a time. In the dream there were men and women whirling in ceremonial dress around a child who was lying on the ground, completely silent. Everything was in slow motion, and while it could have been a peaceful scene, there was something wrong about it. It struck the man as more of a warning and less of a dream; almost as if there were clues he was supposed to follow in order to understand the basic nature of the scene playing out before him.

The child, an infant, was watching the procession with understanding in its eyes, as if it already knew what the dance was for, and why it was being performed. There was something ritualistic to the movements; an appeasement dance perhaps, or a dance to ward off some unseen evil spirit. An itch at the back of the man's head told him there was something familiar with the scene, something more than simply a dream, but then he had awakened. It had happened as soon as he was noticed as a bystander of the dance. And, as dreams most often do, the details had begun to fade the moment the man's eyes adjusted to the darkness in his room. Most dreams of this nature drifted out of the head completely, and this one was no exception, until the man watched the swirling autumn leaves gracefully descend to the earth below.

The man wanted the dream out of his head, so he physically tried to shake it away. It worked enough to his satisfaction, and he moved down the street and turned into the driveway of a small brown house. The man was in his late forties, wore a nondescript brown sports coat over a black tee, and finished the ensemble with dark blue jeans and a pair of Vans. He carried himself with a confident air of self-knowledge; one that informed anyone around him that he knew precisely what he was doing.

He approached the front door of the house and stood there for a moment, gathering himself, before rapping lightly on the door. The man had been on many of these calls, and they had always ended the same way. *Thank you very much and a nice day to you too.* No matter how tense the situations became, the man never lost his temper, as most people he visited were apt to do when they found out what the man thought of their, how to put it lightly, ridiculous attempts at fortune and fame. After the person would undoubtedly refer to the man as a 'false prophet in need of a good ass whooping,' or some other affectation in that vein but usually more ribald in nature, it was always *Thank you very much and a nice day to you too.*

The man had specific rituals that he observed; not that he was superstitious by any means, but certain constants can help a person grope his way through the day-to-day.

After about a minute the door was opened by a haggard man with dark half-moon shadows beneath his eyes. Most likely he was in his late thirties, but could have passed for early sixties, and he stared out at the man before welcoming him into his home. This man was John

Billings, a single father of two young children, aged 4 and 6, and the owner of a lifetime supply of pity and well-wishes from the locals because his wife had passed two months prior. The man decided he would allow Mr. Billings to be the first to break the silence, and followed him into the living room, where the children sat in front of the television, watching some cartoon with a young man and his dog who appeared to be battling an old wizard king. Neither of them turned when their dad and the strange man entered the room.

Mr. Billings sighed deeply, closed his eyes for a few seconds—the man noticed a tear clinging to the edge of Mr. Billings' left eye, and waited for it to fall, which it never did—and then gestured to the recliner. The man took the seat and Mr. Billings finally broke the terrible, sad silence. "It's Grimm, right?"

"Marcus Grimm," the man replied softly. "You can call me Marcus. That's fine."

"Marcus. I'm John. Can I get you something to drink? We don't have much I'm afraid. Tap water, milk, tea, or something a little stronger?" The sadness in John's voice was deep. It wrapped around him and squeezed into his core. Marcus made a mental note to leave a therapist's number just in case this sorrow had wound its way into John's soul.

"I would love some tap water, thank you," John said quietly. He hadn't really wanted the water, and likely the glass would sit next to him untouched until long after he had left, but he wanted a moment to observe the two children in the room.

At first assessment both of them looked clean and well kept. It appeared that the older sibling was a girl, and the younger a boy. The biological resemblance was too great for them to not be blood related. Both had their father's slightly sloping nose that opened at the nostril end asymmetrically, one hole slightly more open than the other. The girl had dark brown hair, and the boy's was a dirty blonde that may have been more strawberry when he was a baby. The dream came unbidden into his mind of the infant lying in the middle of the spinning dancers, and Marcus had to blink the vision away.

Neither of the children so much as glanced his way, which he took as either a sign that they had no reason to mistrust anyone who came through that front door, or that they were told to ignore the man who was coming to the house unless they were called upon to give witness before God and man to the things their father was telling to Mr. Marcus. Marcus felt it was the former, and he relaxed a little.

Once, he had visited a house where the father seemed on edge the entire visit, and the child, no older than five, had been watching television. The little boy did not glance even one time at Marcus; didn't take his eyes off the TV for even a split second. But Marcus had noticed that every few seconds a tear slid down his cheek dripping off his chin onto his dirty t-shirt.

Marcus watched as the boy lifted an arm to wipe away one of his tears and saw finger shaped bruises on the underside of the child's arm. He excused himself to the bathroom, called CPS, and then stalled the man until they showed up with an officer.

Child Protective Services took the boy from his father who, after admitting to a jury of peers his heinous dealings with his son, ended up in prison. Not long after, while sitting in his cell, reading a book quietly, two men entered and literally stuck it to him until he bled out. According to an anonymous witness two nearby guards physically turned from the cell and put in earbuds moments before the attack. They were given two weeks paid vacation and returned to their posts with no further repercussions. The anonymous tipper was transferred to another prison in case the guards decided to punish him for snitching. All of that was purely speculative, of course.

That was one of those cases where Marcus saying, "Thank you very much and a nice day to you too," was his way of sticking with ritual to keep himself from pounding his fists into the man's face repeatedly. Marcus was a very forgiving person, but he did not abide the cowardice of a grown human attacking a child.

John broke through the reminiscing. "Are you all right, Mr. Grimm?"

It took Marcus a moment to recognize that John was speaking to him, and another moment to realize he was squeezing the armrests of the recliner a little too tightly. He forced himself to relax and saw finger shaped indentations (bruises) on the chair. With not a little amount of effort, Marcus smiled up at John. "Sorry, I was remembering an unpleasant memory." *Thank you very much and a nice day to you too.*

John studied Marcus for a moment, and Marcus could see a deep intelligence in his eyes. He was truly sizing Marcus up in a way that slightly unnerved him. After a few seconds of silence he nodded his head slightly and sat down on the sofa. For a moment Marcus thought John was going to keep sinking into the couch until he was nestled in next to the loose change and food wrappers undoubtedly embedded in the under part of the cushions. John *did* end up sitting lower than Marcus, but the loose change was safe for the moment.

"So, the website said you deal with this type of…uh," he hesitated, searching for the right word to use, and his eyes focused slightly when he found it, "phenomena."

Phenomena seemed a tad intense to Marcus, considering over ninety percent of the people that hired him to investigate their cases ended up being frauds. In fact, most of the parents he met in his line of work were looking for a get rich quick scheme, hoping to fool Marcus into corroborating their stories. Almost without fail, he could sniff out the ruse within five minutes of entering someone's house, and he would take his fee, along with a tongue lashing and some veiled, or not-so veiled, threats before leaving the house in his dust. *Thank you and a nice day to you too.*

The young boy with the bruises had been a *five minutes or less* home. It had been, to be honest, open and shut before Marcus had made friends with the seat cushion. Normally he didn't dwell on that case, but for some reason everything reminded him of it today. He made a note to call CPS and check on the kid. Brandon had been his name; or was it Braden. Whichever it was, CPS would know who he was referencing with a few key words. Marcus felt John's gaze on him and realized he had not responded in some time. "Basically. That's a broad term, and to be honest, most cases are phony."

John thought about the response for a few seconds, and then picked his next question carefully. "Are you a charlatan, Mr. Grimm?" He winced after asking it.

Marcus felt the right side of his mouth lift into a quiet smile and thought to himself, *Well, officer, that's when he pulled out his ten-dollar words and I felt insecure about myself, so I beat him with a shoe.* John stared at him intently, waiting for him to answer, and Marcus realized the longer he didn't answer the question the more likely Mr. Billings was betting that he was, in fact, a phony. "Not to my knowledge, Mr. Billings."

"Please, it's John." The response was simple but put Marcus's mind at ease: If the man still insisted on a first-name basis, he probably believed Marcus on some level.

And it was true. Marcus *was* no charlatan. He had no idea where his intuition came from or how he so accurately predicted outcomes or unexpected moves from people, but he had long ago put away the notion that he was just one lucky sumbitch.

The first time he realized he had a gift was in the third grade. He was waiting for his father to pick him up outside of the school's entrance. An image flashed through his mind of someone, a man who was balding and had a yellow snaggletooth, telling him his mom has asked him to take Marcus home. The stranger was unaware that Marcus and his father had developed a codeword for such instances, let alone that his mother was dead. "Listen up, bucko," his father had said with a slight grin on his face, "If someone ever comes up to you and says they are there to take you home, but you don't recognize that person, make them tell you the codeword. If they don't know it, you scream and run like the dickens." Something in Marcus told him this was happening. It was game time. This man was going to come and try to steal him away.

He only had to wait two minutes before the man pulled up in a panel van and leaned out the passenger window. "Yer ma told me to come pick ya up. She been in a accident and I'm gonna take ya up ta the hospital."

And when he flashed a nasty grin there was that gross yellow snaggletooth in all its glory. For a moment Marcus could only stare, and then he opened his mouth and screamed as loud as he could and ran into the school. The van left long tire marks on the pavement in the speedy getaway. Someone would later remark on how maybe Doc and Marty had come by on one of their time travel adventures.

After that instance, Marcus trusted his brain's eye. That's what he called it. And his brain's eye had a near perfect record. The only problem he had encountered was when he was drunk or too emotionally involved; then the brain's eye would alter small (or not so small) details. His brain's eye had even saved his life on several occasions. *Thank you and a nice day to you too.*

"Well, John," Marcus said, coming out of his reverie. "I understand the inherent desire to be skeptical. And, honestly, I trust someone who is skeptical of my...abilities more than I trust someone who welcomes me with open arms and agrees with everything I say." John was nodding his head. "So, I will make the same promises I make to everyone who hires me, and you can decide if you want to engage my services. Sound fair?"

Again, John nodded his head. "Fair."

"Here are my three promises." He ticked them off on his fingers as he went along. "Number one, I will not razzle-dazzle you. I'm not going to make anything move, I'm not going to go into a trance-like state and conjure up dead people, and I'm not going to suddenly feel super cold. Two, I will give you my honest assessment of the situation, which, most of the time ends up that whatever is happening is false, or a charade. And three, I will not promise you more information for more money, meaning I'm not going to extort you for your cash. Does that suit you fine?"

If Marcus wasn't mistaken, it looked as if John was slightly disappointed that there would be no physical manifestations of the spirit world.

John studied Marcus carefully for a minute and then looked at his children. "I think that sounds good. I just want to know what is happening with my kids."

Marcus furrowed his brow and nodded curtly. "Let's get to work, shall we?

CHAPTER 2

John told Marcus that his children's names were Charlie and Cynthia, that they had always been normal kids, nothing out of the ordinary to stick a pin into for later examination. They enjoyed their TV shows and board games and the same five songs they insisted on listening to on repeat until it was stuck in dear ol' dad's head for the next week. And of course, they fought on occasion—they were siblings after all—but never hurt each other.

It was at this time that John became a little nervous.

"I want to show you something," John continued, "but I want you to know that I, one-hundred percent, would never hurt my kids; either of them." John let out a nervous little laugh. "I bet you hear that from a lot of people who end up being the ones that hurt their kids." He stared off into space for a moment, seemingly composing himself, and when he returned his gaze to Marcus, he smiled, but looking dreadfully tired.

Marcus stayed still and silent, trying not to make a judgment, but already sirens in his brain's eye started to sound, not loudly but present. He wasn't alarmed yet, but he was ready if the need arose.

When Marcus didn't react, John took a deep breath and looked at his son. "Charlie, can you come over here for a minute, bud?"

The boy stood up and turned, and for the first time Marcus saw his eyes. They looked haunted, as if Charlie's eyes didn't really belong to him, but were a conduit for something or someone else to see through.

Thoughts came rapid-fire to Marcus and even as he tried to push them to the side, they still sat in the corner of his mind much like a kid in timeout who won't stop asking if the punishment is done yet.

John held out his hand to Charlie and said softly, "I want you to show Mr. Grimm your ankle."

Charlie's eyes darted to Marcus and then back to his dad. After only a moment's hesitation and a nodded confirmation from his father, Charlie lifted his pant leg slightly and Marcus could see the scratches on his ankle. They were red and starting to scab over, and Marcus guessed it had happened no more than a few days prior to this meeting.

Marcus knelt in front of the chair, feeling his age as both his knees crackled, and looked more intently at the scratches. Holding out his hand he looked up at Charlie, "These old knees of mine. I'm surprised I can even move around anymore."

He smiled kindly at Charlie, but the boy stared through him. Marcus gestured to the ankle. "May I?"

Another quick glance to his dad and Charlie held it out for Marcus to examine.

Taking the boy's ankle gently in his hand, Marcus traced the scabby marks with his fingertips. It looked as though someone with long nails had tried to grab hold of his ankle and Charlie had yanked free of the grasp, but not without consequences.

For a few moments, Charlie allowed Marcus to examine the wound but, becoming nervous, pulled his leg out of reach, turned and sat back down in front of the television next to his sister, who absently reached out and took his hand. Marcus sensed a strong connection between the siblings.

"Have you talked to his teachers to see if he is being bullied at school?" Marcus was gentle in tone, but the question still felt callous coming off his lips.

"He doesn't start pre-school until the Spring. He isn't around a lot of other kids. Not since their mom..." John trailed off as his eyes darted toward his children.

"I'm sorry to have to ask..." Marcus began warily.

Thankfully, he didn't have to finish the question, because John anticipated and answered, "Oh God no! I would never harm my children. I already told you that."

Marcus nodded his head. "I believe you. There are usually signs from the children, subconscious mostly, that hint at domestic abuse, but your children don't seem to exhibit any of those markers."

John let out a forced breath. A tear glistened in the corner of his eye, which he quickly blinked away. Marcus could tell he feared something but getting to the bottom of that fear would only be relevant if it was related to possible paranormal happenings surrounding Charlie or Cynthia.

Marcus was beginning to sense an energy, a sort of aura, surrounding the family, but there was conflict in the feeling; a duality that was confusing. One wave of information set him at ease and felt like a flowing river with a soft breeze; another wave felt as if a hand was gripping his heart constricting it, making it difficult to breathe and think clearly. Joy and anger, peace and turmoil, love and hate swirling altogether in an invisible orb that made Marcus weary. He emerged from his thoughts as John asked him a question, which Marcus then asked him to repeat.

"I was just asking what type of information you need from us," John repeated slowly.

"Has there been any death in the family recently? You mentioned your wife." He asked the question, watching John's face intently for any indicators of trauma involved with the deceased.

"Their mother died only a couple months ago. She had lung cancer, and it was very aggressive, late stage. The doctors couldn't do anything." John's face contorted as though the mental and emotional strain of talking about his wife was twisting him from the inside out. He saw that Marcus was focused entirely on him and worked to return to normal. After a couple deep breaths, John seemed a little better, and then continued. "I always felt like there was a little more the doctors could have done, but they assured me over and over that my wife was destined for eternity. I am doing my best with these kids, but sometimes I feel like I'm failing them."

Marcus felt a pang of compassion stab his heart, and he nearly reached out and touched John's arm, but he held himself back. "You seem to be doing a fine job," Marcus heard his mouth saying, before he could stop himself. *Step 1: Don't get emotionally involved with the family.* "Any other deaths?"

John's lips pursed as he thought about the correct answer to that. "No one else in our immediate family. My brother passed away about a year ago, but he hardly ever visited."

"Were you close?" Marcus tried to navigate the question with caution, but sometimes there was no way around spitting up the question like so much bile. "Did he ever harm your children?"

John looked genuinely surprised by the question. "Jesus! No!" He regained his composure. "Sorry. I, just...no, he would never hurt my kids."

Marcus looked at John sympathetically. "Again, I have to ask. The more information I have, the better I can assess if something paranormal is happening in the house."

"You think it's the house that's haunted?" John looked like he had been waiting to ask the question since Marcus arrived.

"I can't say that for certain yet. Once I have more information, we can start to make slight assumptions. Then we can test those assumptions to find if there is any validity to them. Think of it as the scientific method, but with the paranormal world." Marcus tried to smile, but it felt hollow. He had begun to feel that intuition pit in his brain's eye start to grow.

Even as a child Marcus had always been a good judge of character. Some say that children are inherently gifted with bullshit detectors, but Marcus's seemed to be sharper than most. His parents learned very quickly that if Marcus was uncomfortable around someone there was a reason. More than a few times his discernment helped them get out of awkward situations, and later they would read about a murder in the newspaper with a photo identifying the potential killer, the very person Marcus "pointed out" to them shortly before.

Marcus hadn't been much of a reader growing up, but when he found himself drawn to Stephen King novels. The idea of intuition, or *The Shining*, as King described it, had fascinated Marcus, and he felt like at least one person understood his ability at a base level. However, he wouldn't say that he had *The Shining*, as much as an ability to read people. He had described it as detecting an off giving of aura. Everyone had colors associated with their auras; some people were bright, rainbow colored, while others were duller and grayer. In his lifetime he had only encountered one individual who seemed to be giving off an inky black viscous color thicker than oil, but that had only happened once when he was a teenager. The street where he met this person is the only street he avoided at all costs.

Another piece of the puzzle that Marcus found remarkably similar to King novels was the concept of *The Thin Place*; places on earth where the physical and spiritual realms almost exist side-by-side. In these places you could almost reach out and touch the spiritual world if you knew how to look, most often out of the corner of the eye. The concept of *The Thin Place* was not a King original, but he had made very good use of the notion throughout the years. *Thin Places* originated in Celtic mythology and enough people claim to have witnessed them that there might be actual credence to the theory.

Marcus felt that where there was great spiritual conflict the veil thinned to almost transparent. The desperation of a spirit or entity could cause the boundary to drop completely. This is where one might see a poltergeist, or some type of demonic possession or indwelling occur. His job was to find such thinly veiled places and both expose and restore them. Some felt it was needful to communicate with dead relatives, loved ones, pets, even famous people on occasion, but what they always failed to recognize was that opening a portal to the spiritual world wasn't like making a telephone call; it was more like folding a piece of paper multiple times, cutting a hole through it, and unfolding it again. No one in the physical plane has the ability to control what came through those holes, or where.

If Aunt Suzy wanted to contact Uncle Jerry, she might go to a medium, someone who could communicate across the thin place. Whether or not a fraud, they would often offer a séance to communicate with the dead. Let's assume the medium is not a shyster but has a real connection with the "otherworld". She begins the séance, connects with dearly departed Uncle Jerry, and Aunt Suzy is able to have the conversation she always wanted, but couldn't because of that drunk driver. Assuming all of these variables, the medium cuts a hole in the fabric between worlds. Maybe down the street, maybe across town, or in another country, that hole opens a portal to a more malevolent spirit; one that doesn't have any interest in telling his living wife that the money he had been storing away was under the third floorboard in the guest bathroom. There is no facilitator for this new presence, so it is able to run amok and do whatever it pleases, within the bounds of unwritten existential rules, which, of course, are a gray area at best.

One of these "rules" dictates that anyone who opens themselves up willingly to the spiritual world via séance, incantation, or any other form of ritual 'magic' sends out an invitation that they are a viable host for infestation, harassment, or possession. Think vampire: a vampire is not allowed to enter a dwelling unless they are given permission and whatever ritual is performed is the permission granted to any and all spirits.

There are innocence clauses, but they are just as muddied as everything else. In some aspects of conservative Christianity there is an expression, "The Age of Accountability." If a child dies before a certain age, they will automatically go to heaven because they do not have the capacity to make a salvation decision for themselves. However, if you ask those who believe in this concept what the age is, you will get differing answers; it's unclear, akin to trying to see the bottom of a lake while someone throws rocks into it.

Similarly, if a bunch of school friends get out a Ouija Board and start messing with it out of curiosity, people like to believe there is some level of *Age of Accountability* that prevents them from opening themselves up to the spirit world. Others would argue that once you are able to understand there is a spiritual world you have automatically reached that accountable age. Marcus fell in with this line of thought. He believed that if you open yourself up to the spirit world no matter your age, you would always have a connection to that world. Such was the authority of being human, whether you knew it or not.

That being said, Marcus also believed that children were much stronger than adults, because imagination played a significant role in recognizing the spirit world. Once, he had worked with a family whose two-year-old would stare at one corner of the room in the bedroom and smile. Children don't know what name to put on something until someone gives it to them, so the parents asked her if she was seeing angels. She would nod her head and continue to smile. They began to test the theory that their daughter was really seeing *angels* by asking her where her angel was, and daddy's angel was, and mommy's angel was, and then repeating the questions in different orders to try and confuse her. She would correctly respond, pointing out each person's angel always in the same spot of the room. Marcus witnessed this process for himself but had been asked to leave when the parents asked the child where Mr. Grimm's angel was. Their daughter's face had instantly darkened, and tears welled up in her eyes. Apparently, Mr. Grimm did not have a friendly angel or positive spiritual guide of any sort, and they were not pleased. *Thank you very much and a nice day to you too.*

Children saw things that adults did not because children believed in their imaginations. Animals reacted to the spiritual world in a similar way, only they not only saw spirits, they also felt the atmospheric disturbances in the world to such a degree that they knew when catastrophe was about to strike. Dogs would start acting funny, cats would disappear, birds would chirp incessantly, and then a day or two later there would be an earthquake, tornado, or flash flood. They noticed the slight metaphysical changes within the earth, and it resonated with them on an incorporeal level.

Of course, many people cry foul, perhaps because they either lack imagination or adhere to a strictly materialistic perspective where one can only believe objective and provable fact. "If it can't be proven it can't be real." Those same people tend to react negatively when anyone points out that most scientific "facts" were believed before they were proven. They were always real, but until current unproven ideas are proven empirically, it is easier to be a critic.

Marcus smiled at the thought, and then noticed John staring at him. This seemed to be happening a lot this visit. Normally, Marcus was focused and able to get in and out within an hour, even when there was some sort of spiritual energy present. But in this house, he felt particularly distracted, unfocused, and claustrophobic. He figured that might be the cause for the intuition pit. Whatever it was seemed strong, and he hoped he had the energy to withstand it.

He looked over at John and said, "Before I talk to either of your children, I would like to walk the house and property. To survey both the interior and exterior are important to discern if there are any boundaries, or hot spots."

John looked at his children, who were still enthralled with whatever cartoon they were watching, and then nodded his head. "We can start with the front yard."

John walked to the front door, opened it, let Marcus walk through first, glanced back at his children, and then followed with a deep sigh.

CHAPTER 3

They began the tour of the property at the mailbox, John skeptically watching Marcus, as if to say, *You really think some spirit is haunting the mailbox?* Marcus ignored it and focused his energy on feeling for any spikes in the metaphysical. Now that he was truly focusing, he could feel a low voltage hum surrounding the entire property; it was the only way he could describe the sense. Electrical conduits tended to give off a low hum, and if you got too close you could feel the hairs on your body raise slightly due to the static charge. This was what it felt like when there was a nearby spiritual force, and Marcus found it usually to be mostly a pleasant sensation, but when there was an – he didn't want to call it evil, but it was the easiest, most universally known term – evil presence, the hum could grow into the sensation one might get just prior to being struck by lightning. That was one of his gauges for what he was dealing with at any particular job site. Here he was feeling the warm, fuzzy hum, but that only meant that even at the fringes of the property there was still a bit of a presence.

Marcus and John proceeded to walk down the driveway toward the garage and turned toward the front yard that curved around the left side of the house. There was a large oak tree with a tire swing, and a few saplings around the perimeter of the yard. Marcus noticed two bicycles, one with training wheels, and one without, lying in the grass near the swing, looking as though they hadn't been used in months. The rain had rusted the frames, and the helmets seemingly tossed aside, were cracked and full of dirt. John nonchalantly tipped over each helmet with his foot, dumping excess water onto the lawn.

They then walked around the side of the house across a little patch of grass between the home and the fence, and John opened the chain link gate that separated the front yard from the back. It squawked in protest at being disturbed, and John mumbled something about oil, but obviously wasn't trying to make conversation.

When they both passed through the gate, John shut it as quietly as he could, but still loud enough to send a couple birds flying out of a plum tree in the backyard. Here there were a variety of fruit trees, Marcus recognizing an apple, pear, and cherry tree. But wherever there was fruit, it was overripe, and maggots crawled in and out of the flesh like parasites in a wound. He inhaled sharply, and then, trying to control his mind and focus, let the breath out very slowly.

Marcus suddenly realized the low voltage hum had been rising inside him. This put him on edge and made him jumpy. It was as if someone had attached jumper cables to him and had their finger on the switch that would release a charge, and he felt himself anticipating the shock.

Closing his eyes for a moment he gathered his thoughts, re-centering himself, and trying to re-focus again. Even so he felt a swoon that tore at his concentration and for the first time since arriving a darkness began to embrace him. Before he knew what was happening, his whole body convulsed as if something extremely cold had quickly passed through him. He glanced over at John who obviously had noticed and was now looking distinctively nervous.

After a few moments of deep breathing and attempting to regain his composure, Marcus scanned the backyard, which was mostly barren. There were a couple raised beds overrun by weeds and some small plants near the fence line, all either dead or well on their way. He noticed a shed in the far corner of the yard and made his way toward it.

Opening it, he immediately noticed there were multiples of the same tools, lined up with great care. It reminded him of going to *Home Depot* where all the tools were hung from racks: Three shovels, three rakes, three axes, in fact, everything he could see was in threes. John broke the tension by chuckling behind him. "My wife always said I was a pack rat. I never was good at letting things go, and I like to be prepared."

The wording struck Marcus as odd, so he pursued it a bit, trying to hide his questioning with humor. "Preparing for the zombie apocalypse?"

John laughed again. "Nah. If one of my tools breaks, I don't want to have to stop what I'm doing in order to go buy a new one. You know how it is."

Marcus nodded his head courteously and went back to examining the tools. Each looked brand new, and not one was even slightly out of place. He imagined if he opened the toolbox, he would find the same thing with hammers, screwdrivers, and everything else. For a second, he wondered if the nails and screws were kept in multiples of three, and brushed the thought away, but not before a private smile curled his lips. He took a step deeper into the shed and felt the hum grow to a buzz; one he could feel rising from his chest and into his head. Alarm bells began ringing, and Marcus made a mental note to return to this outbuilding later if he wasn't getting the information he needed inside the house. For the moment he acted as if nothing had happened and backed his way out.

They walked the short distance to the back door to the garage, and Marcus and John walked into a two-car space as neat and tidy as the toolshed. In one corner he spied an arts and crafts area where the kids undoubtedly let their creative sides roam free. Unexpectedly, the moment John closed the door behind them the hum almost completely dissipated. *This is a safe place,* Marcus thought to himself. It's good there is at least one in this house.

Safe spaces were not rare in houses where something paranormal was occurring. Movies often portrayed that once a spirit was within a house there was no hiding from it, and even if the family leaves, the spirit tends to follow. Although this was true in some cases, nine times out of ten there was always at least one safe space within a home. It might be a closet, bathroom, attic, garage, or any other place. There are theories why such places exist, places where spirits refuse to go, but like most theory regarding the supernatural they were mostly guess and conjecture.

Marcus's own theory on why spirits don't enter certain areas had to do with his belief that there existed both immensely powerful positive spiritual forces and equally commanding negative spiritual forces. Most spirits fell into the in-between of the two extremes, so if there was a positive spirit in a house and a room where great evil was perpetrated, they could not enter that area of the house, and vice-versa. If a negative spirit encountered a room that had been anointed with holy oil or had been prayed over, they were not able to enter; more gray rules of the spiritual realm that Marcus hoped he understood more than most. He himself had never invited a spirit to commune with him, so he could only make best guesses at what truly was happening in the interactions between the physical and spiritual. Regardless, he sincerely had no desire to ever attempt to "dance with devils" as he put it; he had witnessed the consequences of such trysts and it wasn't even on the edges of temptation.

Marcus wavered in one spot for a moment, feeling something akin to pleasure rise through his legs and into his groin. To anyone else, it might look like he was experiencing the beginnings of arousal, but *this* feeling was quite different. It rose through his abdomen to his chest and finally settled in his head, almost as if a very potent and pleasant mind-altering drug had been administered. This continued for a few seconds, if that, and then was gone. After it had dissipated, and this wasn't the first time he had the experience, he had difficulty explaining the exact nature of the sensation. Euphoric was the closest anyone had come to truly describing it, but even that did it no true justice. It simply was, and then wasn't. *Thank you very much and a nice day to you too.* But this particular experience truly defined the term 'a nice day'.

John continued to stare at Marcus, and without looking back, out of the corner of his eye Marcus could see that John was conflicted, questioning his decision to hire him in the first place. He allowed the emotional wave to pass through his body completely, and once his mind was back in the right place he smiled at John and simply explained, "There are a lot of odd things that take place between realms. There are moments I feel them more deeply." And that is where he left it. And that is where John seemed to leave it as well.

They continued into the house through the garage door connected to the kitchen. Marcus didn't feel as if he needed to waste too much time in areas where he had already been, but he purposefully allowed himself focus and tune in for a few moments, to see if he picked anything else up that was of interest.

When he stood in the living room behind and between the children, he felt the intense tug-of-war again. As trite as it might seem, the easiest description was a battle between good and evil. In reality it was much more convoluted than that, but most people didn't care for "convoluted" or nuance. *Just tell me that one side is righteous, and one side is damned* a father had once intoned to him, his voice quavering slightly.

To the man's credit, his life had come to a screeching halt when he was informed that a drunk driver had smashed into his wife's car. He overheard the paramedics say, "The grease stain went almost as far as the blood stain." His wife had been driving, with their four-year-old in the backseat. Worse, the man later found out their second child was nestled securely inside its womb, minding its own business.

Marcus didn't blame the man for the action he took after finding out this third piece of the garbled mess of a puzzle he was assembling: with clear resolve and proving himself of sound mind, he went to a gun dealer, found the drunk driver – who, surprise, surprise, had walked away with hardly a scratch – and emptied two clips into him while he was sleeping off a night at the bar. The man then turned the gun on himself. *One side is righteous, and one side is damned.* It is never that simple.

When the police searched his home, they found an autosaved letter the man had been typing but had never finished. Or maybe he had. All it said in the center of the screen was:

I guess we're all damned, eh Grimm?

Detectives questioned Marcus, and it took a lot of explaining before they even began to grasp what he did for a living. *The man wanted me to see if his wife and son were in the house still with him. He thought he felt their presence.* After lots of rolled eyes and raised eyebrows, they let him go.

But Marcus was used to such encounters. He sometimes wondered if *he* would believe a word he said if put in their shoes; probably not.

The whirling dervish images inexplicably returned to his thoughts along with a rising, illogical fear that the baby in the center would be stepped on and trampled, a grease stain almost as far as the blood stain. When the vision flashed, he experienced an uncontrollable knee-jerk reaction. His muscles tensed, abdomen flexed, and his eyes scanned as if he could find the baby and protect it. But all that was in front of him was John and his two children. Children who had yet to even acknowledge that a strange man was wandering through their home.

John held out his hand, gesturing toward the back of the house, to the bedrooms. Marcus thought he saw a slight cringe from Charlie, but it may have just been a clinch response to whatever cartoon he was ingesting.

Marcus was aware that when kids watched media they didn't simply observe. They drank it in, swallowing information, knowledge, and behavioral paradigms. Children were like sponges. One might think they were mindlessly watching a TV show or movie, but truly their souls were soaking up so much more. An evidence of this was when a child said something the parent didn't even remember mentioning, only to realize the phrase was from a show they had been watching weeks earlier. There were times that Marcus thought the downfall of society wouldn't be the fighting and bickering among adults, but the underestimation of the capability and intelligence of children.

He considered himself childlike in this regard, having retained the ability to soak up mixed messages. He had an unusual penchant for intuition, and ideas and concepts came easily. In a room full of people from various backgrounds at differing stages in their lives, he could intuit where their experiences had taken them with astonishing accuracy. Some people might put him in the category of psychic, but Marcus preferred to think of it as observational overkill. It was this skill that also garnered him looks like the ones he was getting from John.

Almost impatiently, John gestured again toward the back of the house and Marcus's feet moved. No sooner had they stepped out of the main living space than Marcus's head felt like it was going to explode. Something had reached inside his skull and was aggressively squeezing his brain. And then a whisper of a voice: *Leave this place*. With that the pressure was gone.

Marcus instinctively reached up to his nose to check if it was bleeding, but there was nothing. John put a hand on his shoulder and said something, but Marcus was still recovering and didn't hear him. John's voice was muffled, as if Marcus were under a foot of water and John was yelling to him from the surface. He opened his mouth twice, as if trying to pop his ears, and then the feeling was gone for good; another occurrence nearly impossible to describe once it departed.

"Are you all right, Mr. Grimm?" John repeated, looking concerned.

Marcus nodded and slowly replied, "I am fine. Just hit a wall of something. I don't know what..." or *who*, he thought, "...it was, but I now believe the bedroom section of your house has the strongest energy. I want you to be prepared, but things might go a little sideways. Don't worry, I've dealt with sideways many times." He slapped a grin on his face that he hoped looked sincere to John.

Although looking apprehensive, John seemed satisfied enough with Marcus's answer, and they continued down the hall. They stopped outside the first bedroom, looking inside. Obviously, the room was Cynthia's: pictures of ponies, toy horses, pink cowboy hat, a My Little Pony bedspread; the place looked like a miniature ranch for magical horses.

"This is Charlie's room," John blurted out, ending with a forced laugh. When he saw that Marcus looked absolutely stunned, he apologetically said, "Just a joke. Trying to relieve the tension. It's Cynthia's room."

Marcus felt like he should acknowledge John and his joke, but the pull of Cynthia's room was so entrancing he couldn't concentrate long enough to put the man at ease. He smelled lavender and cardamom, and something else he couldn't quite place. There was a glow in the room that prismed out every time he tried to focus on it; the space was bright, but no lights were on in the physical world. He took a deep breath, stepped inside, and was immediately lost. His eyes closed, but he could see everything: wildflowers growing in a thicket, a family of deer grazing lazily by a creek, the fawn had twelve spots along its back, a man-made path winding through the woods, and a family setting up a picnic complete with checkered blanket. Marcus had never felt so at peace. He watched as the family set out utensils, plates, food, and drink, and then the mother turned to him and smiled, and knocked Marcus back into the house where he was standing in the physical world.

This time when he raised his fingers to his nose, he found that he *was* bleeding. He looked around and saw John standing next to him with a tissue in his hand. "What just happened?" he asked tentatively.

"I don't know," Marcus began. "But it was strong."

John stood silent for a moment, and it looked as though he were debating saying what he was thinking. "Uh, your eyes glazed over, and you counted from one to twelve, and then you were back, or here, I mean present again."

Marcus tried to come up with some explanation for what happened, but he didn't really know. It was like no other experience he had ever had. The reality of it was so vivid he thought he could have grabbed a clump of grass and brought it back with him. He took a deep breath, but the smell of lavender and cardamom had dissipated. The room was empty, at least for the moment.

Marcus turned to John and said, "I would like to see Charlie's room now."

Charlie's room was directly across the hall from his sister's. Before stepping into the room Marcus took another deep breath. He wasn't sure what to expect this time, but the dual between spirits he had been feeling since he arrived didn't give him much hope to revisit the smell of lavender and cardamom and take a stroll through the forest.

His left foot entered the room, followed by his right. And he felt…nothing. Nothing at all. But that wasn't quite right. The room felt like it had been evacuated. It was as if someone had come in and done a clean sweep in order to show off a place pristine and pure. Antiseptic. There was a false sterility about it, and Marcus sniffed the air, half expecting to smell disinfectant. But nothing. Nothing at all.

He felt a sudden urge to walk back to Charlie, grab his hands, and see if there were callouses, as if he had worked extraordinarily hard to make this place look perfect. It was a ridiculous notion; the antiseptic feel of the room was coming from the incorporeal side.

Otherwise, the boy's room was ordinary, even perfectly messy. A half-built LEGO set on his desk, a comic book on his nightstand, and action figures strewn throughout. The bed wasn't made, and clothes littered the floor. It took Marcus a moment to realize that it was a little advanced for a four-year-old to be building sophisticated LEGOs, but he assumed John had been helping him with that task.

As he stepped deeper into the room, Marcus caught a single flash of instability. It was like a ripple in a lake. The glassy purity of the room was disturbed for an instant, and then it went back to the complete calm. It seemed to Marcus as if he had been given the opportunity to peek behind the curtain for a mere second, like the person who did the cleaning was coming in to make sure they hadn't left anything conspicuous behind. He ignored the ripple for the moment, but he now believed that his suspicions of two spirits in the house were nearly confirmed.

Marcus knew he wouldn't get anything else out of Charlie's room for the time being, so he walked out, John quickly on his heels, as if he didn't want to be in his son's room. *Maybe that's why the LEGO set is only half done. John doesn't like being in the room.* The thought came unbidden to Marcus, and he glanced at John, noticing that his face had taken on a slightly ashen quality.

There was one room left, and it was the Master Bedroom. Marcus glanced in the hall bathroom, but it seemed like the most normal room of the house, so he didn't linger. He stepped up to the door of the Master Bedroom and tentatively put his hand on the knob. When nothing happened, he let out a relieved sigh. John looked at him but said nothing.

They stepped into the room and Marcus was not surprised to find that it was fairly sparse. There are typically two types of widowers; those who can't get rid of their dead spouse's belongings, and those who go through the house the day after the funeral and purge the house of everything. John was the latter, which made Marcus think about his tour of the property. He realized he had not seen a single picture of John's wife, or any of her clothes, or any sign that she had ever lived here. Maybe some of the dishes were hers, but, even if there had been fine China that was special to her, Marcus suspected it was now somewhere else.

There wasn't a lot to look at in John's room; a bed, nightstand, dresser, a TV mounted on the wall, and a little pile of shoes in the corner of the room. Some of the shoes had caked mud on them, which probably meant they were his yard shoes. A little way off from the main pile of shoes was a pair of sneakers that looked like they had the special privilege of extra attention. They looked brand new without a speck of dirt or wear to indicate they had ever been worn. The room was normal, not Charlie's room abnormal normal, but simply vanilla. The carpeting looked fairly new and appeared to be the only aspect of the room that wasn't completely bland.

Marcus nodded his head and turned to John. "Okay, I *will* tell you that there is definitely some energy here. Have you ever felt it yourself? A low, resonant hum that sits in your brain, but you can't seem to find the source?"

John looked down for a moment and furrowed his brow. "I can't say that I have. I *have* noticed the kids on occasion messing with their ears, but I always figured it was an earache or something."

"The other thing I can say right now is it feels like there are two spirits in the house. And they seem to be in conflict with one another." Marcus studied John for any sort of reaction but got none.

"Is one of them my wife?" John asked nonchalantly.

"I can't say for sure, but I am assuming one of them might be." Marcus was purposefully noncommittal with his words. He had learned it was best to be vague until he had more definitive proof of his speculations.

There was a particular case where he mistook the energy in the house for a lost loved one, and when it turned out to be someone who had lived in the house previous to the current owners, and that someone had been murdered in the attic, the people who had hired him were understandably irate.

We communicated with this spirit like it was our Uncle, and now you're telling us that our house is haunted by some pissed off spirit that doesn't want to go to the afterlife? We want our money back.

They were certainly not the angriest he had encounter. And it was just another *Thank you very much and a nice day to you too* moment in the long history of his work. He had given half the money back to the family as a gesture of goodwill, and never again offered too much opinion before it was necessary.

"Here's the thing, John. I don't want to say that it *is* your wife, and then it turns out to be something else entirely and you get upset with me."

Marcus surprised himself with his stark honesty. He usually wasn't one for spilling the beans, but here he was, in this house, feeling as though the connection was different. For whatever reason, Marcus was unable to professionally disconnect from what was unfolding. Deep in his soul he felt a sense that this case was going to change everything. In what way, Marcus couldn't say, but there was a unique flavor to this house and to his participation. He wasn't sure he liked what he was tasting.

"I need to speak to your children independent of one another."

John's suspicious eye turned again toward Marcus. "Alone?"

Marcus nodded slowly. "Preferably. And I understand the concern. I can conduct the interviews in the garage. We can even open up the garage door if that helps."

Marcus could see John's body stiffen with defensiveness and he admired the man and understood in that moment that this father would never harm his children or allow anyone else to do anything to them. "Why can't I be in the room?"

"When authority figures, especially parents, are in the room or can hear the conversation, people, especially little people, tend to alter their answers. Either they don't want the person to know a piece of the story, or they feel like they will let them down or give away a secret by saying the wrong thing. I am a stranger, so it is safer to tell me those little tidbits than it is you."

"What if they don't know an answer to one of your questions?"

"I don't push the point. I am looking for the truth, so if they genuinely don't know, I don't want to force feed them a reply that isn't wholly theirs."

John looked perplexed, so John continued, "The power of suggestion is very potent, and it can stain the purity of a response to the point where the truth is unattainable. If I ask you whether you locked your car, suggesting you may not have, it is likely you will have that little blossom of panic because you can't remember, even though you always lock your car when you get out of it.

"Children's answers are fairly pure and straightforward because they haven't learned that bluntness is unkind. We raise children to tell the truth, the whole truth, and nothing but the truth, until they spill something embarrassing, and then we teach them to withhold some truths; discretion and all that. And most kids want to impress their parents, so if they can see their mother or father, they will tailor an answer to make them proud or to not disappoint or anger them.

"The other, slightly more cynical reason for individual interviews is there is less chance to get the story straight among all parties involved. This is why police interrogate a crew of suspects separately. Even when they agree to sync storylines, someone almost always slips up; that's why it's so much easier to tell the truth."

"You don't have to remember anything." John put in his two cents. It seemed he wanted Marcus to stop talking. "I got you. All right, I will agree to it, but on two conditions: You sit five feet from my kids, and I get to be right outside the door listening for any signs of distress."

Marcus tried on a smile again, but it still felt fake. "I agree to your terms."

They shook hands and walked back out to where the kids were watching some cartoon about a dog in space. *Rover's Rover* Marcus thought, wondering if that was actually the name of the show.

CHAPTER 4

Marcus looked down at the children, and for a moment wondered if he was going to be able to break the electronic trance they seemed to be under. So, he knelt, feeling again that now too familiar creak in his knees, and winced. As if he needed another reminder of his age. Over the hill is what they said, but he had hoped he would have more time on that upslope before his weak knees made him tumble down the far side. "Charlie, I was wondering if I could talk to you for a few minutes."

Charlie didn't look over. The show was far too engaging.

Marcus put a gentle hand on his shoulder and tried again, "Charlie, you wanna talk about LEGOs?" Nothing.

That was when he looked over and saw that Cynthia was staring him down. He almost jumped backward but managed to keep his composure. "I think I should talk to you first. If that's okay, Mr. Grimm." There was an old-soul air about the girl. He could feel the intelligence in her eyes piercing him like a laser beam. It was intense but respectful.

"I think that would be good, Cynthia. Would you like to talk in the garage?" Marcus noted that something in Cynthia's demeanor relaxed when he mentioned the garage. He suspected she could feel the atmospheric difference in there just as he had.

Marcus stood up, noting that crackle of his knees and vowing to get them checked out when he had time. He held out his hand to Cynthia who took it and as he turned to lead her to the garage, he looked at John, who was staring at Cynthia intently. Her hand dropped from Marcus's in an instant.

That was fine with Marcus, and had, in fact been to test one of his assumptions; to see the reactions. If John were in the room while he talked to Cynthia, she would censor her answers appropriately. Now that he was fully convinced, he could make the conversation run smoothly. He looked at John and mouthed *Five feet. Promise.* And the two entered the garage together.

Marcus looked around and the interview started before Cynthia was even aware of the shift. "Does your dad have any folding chairs out here? I'd like to sit down. I'm old, you know?"

He watched her face, and while she was slightly amused by the thought of his being old, there was sadness and distress behind her eyes.

Over the course of the many years making house calls he had slowly learned how to interact with children of different ages. A star witness could turn into a stone façade if he didn't approach them appropriately. Children who were Cynthia's age needed to be engaged; involved. If they were asked to participate from the start, they felt as though the adult respected them and their ability to make decisions. Often, adults underestimated kids, thinking their fantasies and invisible friends and secret languages were all signs that their brains hadn't yet fully developed. In his experience, it was not unusual for adults to treat children like babies, and the young ones tended to respond accordingly. They might as well live to the expectation this adult had and act like they knew nothing.

Cynthia was slightly different, but not much. He could still see the sparkle of imagination in her eyes, and because of her reserved intelligence, he figured he would have to treat her more like a ten-year-old than a six-year-old. A four-year distinction might not seem like much, but the gap was quite large. As people age, the difference of four years became less and less significant, but in a child it's the difference between playing in a fenced yard and riding your bike through the neighborhood.

They searched for chairs, and Cynthia finally found them stacked behind a shelving unit that held odds and ends that every household acquired over the years. Marcus remembered that he had promised John he'd open the garage door to the outside world, so he grabbed the chairs, set them up five feet from each other, and then hit the open button.

He sat in his seat and Cynthia sat in hers, her legs dangling slightly, barely too short to reach the ground. They waited in silence until the door slid into position above their heads. Cynthia was the first to speak.

"Why are you so far away?" The question surprised Marcus, but it was an astute observation.

"I told your dad that I would give you your space," Marcus replied calmly.

"Oh yeah, because of molesters." Her tone was so matter of fact it slightly unnerved Marcus.

"But you're not going to molester me." It wasn't a question.

"No, I am not. We are simply going to talk. If that's okay with you?"

Marcus wondered if she realized the question was more a way to involve her in the decision-making process, and less a way for her to get out of talking to him. He figured she did because she nodded slightly and crossed her ankles. After a moment of silence, Marcus asked the simplest question first, "Do you know why I'm here?"

"Because my mom died." No hesitation.

"In a way."

"But," Cynthia tried to find the words, struggling to clearly articulate her thoughts. Finally, Marcus saw something click in her eyes and she looked at him with her wise maple brown eyes. "There's more, right? It's not just about my mom."

Marcus's respect for the little girl continued to climb, but he played it nice and cool. *Don't lead the witness, prosecutor!* "What do you mean?"

Again, that faraway look before answering. "My mom died, and there is something weird happening in the house, but—" Out of focus, into focus. "My dad wants to know what it means. Why it's happening."

Marcus nodded. "What weird things are happening in your house, Cynthia?"

"I don't know. Doors open, doors shut. No one is there. But someone is there." The last came out almost as a whisper and she twisted her mouth as if she knew it didn't make a whole lot of sense. "You know what I mean?"

"So, a door will open or shut, and you will go see who it is, and no one is there."

"But not quite. There's someone there, but not there. Have you ever watched Scooby Doo?"

"Ruh roh," Marcus did his best Scooby Doo impression, and Cynthia actually giggled for a moment, putting her hand to her mouth. It lasted only a moment before she sobered up and became serious once again.

"You know how the ghost or monster always tries to get them to go home, but it always ends up being some old man under the sheet or in the costume?"

Marcus nodded with a smile but started to feel a tendril of a chill take hold at the base of his spine. He wasn't sure he wanted to know where she was going with this analogy, but he knew he had to hear it.

"That's kind of what I mean. I will check the door and sometimes there is something in the corner under a sheet or in a costume. But—" Out of focus, into focus. Did Marcus see a little fear rimming her pupils? A slight dilation? "But I don't want to pull off the sheet. And I don't want to take the head off the costume."

Another pause, and now Marcus could feel the unpleasant tingle spreading through all his limbs. The sensation wrapped around his bad knees and squeezed. Then it made its way to his lower abdomen and squeezed harder. And then she said what he had been dreading, "I don't think it's a sheet. Or a costume. There's no old man underneath, because there *is* no underneath."

It took Marcus a moment to untangle his tongue so he could speak again. *Should have brought that water with me*, he thought. "And you have seen these things?" The question felt stupid even as it exited his mouth, but he was already gripped by slowly rising fear. This was foreign territory for him.

Cynthia nodded her head. "Uh huh. They never do anything except stand there. They watch me. Their heads move to keep an eye on me. Sometimes I think they want to do more, but it's like they can't. They're not allowed to."

"Who is stopping them?" A lump was growing in Marcus's throat and he wondered how much longer he would be able to communicate before he could no longer breathe.

Cynthia shrugged. "My mom, I guess."

"You have seen your mom?"

"I talk to her."

Usually, when a child says they talk to their dead parent or dog or sibling or whoever, it is in a praying sense of conversing. If someone talks to Jesus during prayer, they are presumed to have faith. If they talk to a dead loved one it is considered a coping mechanism. The allowances humanity accepts are myriad. You are allowed to talk to special dead people, like the mother of Jesus or a saint who devoted their lives to the church and helping others. But, not to your mother, unless it is a prayer sort of thing.

This all went through Marcus's head while his intuition whispered to him that this was not one of those prayer talks. Cynthia believed she was communicating with her mother. Marcus had an inkling she wasn't bluffing or playing make-believe.

Marcus regained his mental footing, clearing his throat, "What does your mom say?" There were so many questions demanding attention, but he was trying to work as methodically as possible.

Another shrug from Cynthia. "A lot of things. Mostly how much she misses us and loves us. She tells me stories about when she was little like me."

"Is she in the room with us right now?"

Cynthia's eyes flicked to a corner of the garage and then back to Marcus. It was so quick it was almost imperceptible, but it had happened. "She's coming and going. Sometimes she's in here, but then she'll go back in the house for a bit."

"Why does she keep going in the house?" *Is she checking on your brother and dad?* he almost asked. *Please don't lead the witness.* He bit down on his tongue, the question still wanting to be heard.

"She's making sure dad and Charlie are okay." The answers flowed from Cynthia as easily as if he had asked her what her favorite candy was, or what she ate for dinner.

Marcus took a deep breath. The questions from here would only go deeper and he wasn't sure how far.

"The person standing in the corner, the one you described as a ghost or monster, is that your mom?"

Cynthia laughed, but the laugh brought no joy to Marcus. Instead it felt like a claw had been raked down his back. The laugh told him that it was a silly question, which was not encouraging in the slightest. That meant he had been right when he assumed there was more than one presence in the house. There was no way to tell if it was more than two, but it wouldn't surprise him to find a host of them surrounding the area.

Oftentimes, when evil was present it drew other beings – demons, dead spirits, unknown entities – to the area. They fed off each other and grew stronger. He hoped that he was catching the process early enough that there were only a few.

The worst he had witnessed was a case in Iowa, at a small farmhouse outside of Des Moines. He had taken on the work early in his career, when any job seemed like a good one. As soon as he had passed through the front door, he had nearly been knocked unconscious. The swarming buzz that instantly surrounded him was almost too much for him to handle. His eardrums almost burst, his nose began to bleed, and he could hear the whispers from the collective entity infesting the house.

That was the most intense he had ever encountered, and he could only recall bits and pieces of the experience. He was unable to tell people what exactly had happened or how he had defeated the swarm.

According to eyewitness accounts, he had gone into a deep trance and issued an ultimatum, invoking the power of Christ, which he had never done before and hadn't done since.

It wasn't that Marcus was convinced about a higher power; he wasn't as naïve as that. The forces he had encountered weren't higher, but they were powerful. There was enough evidence that something was out there pulling strings on occasion; getting involved when necessary. He simply didn't have enough information on the Protestant or Catholic God to feel like he could invoke His name.

Apparently, he was wrong. But he still had never attempted it again and hoped this case wouldn't be the one where the invocation would bear repeating. The atmosphere in this place wasn't nearly as devastating, but whatever it was could have been prepared, like when he entered Charlie's room.

"Has your mom told you how many others are in the house?" Marcus asked this slowly, hoping he wasn't projecting an idea.

"She says it is just her and one other, but the other is pretty strong." This was the first moment where Cynthia looked scared, and Marcus didn't like it. He almost went up and hugged her to reassure her that everything was going to be all right, but if he betrayed John's trust now the fight would be over before it began.

"Does she know if the other entity is a person or something else?" Again, he asked the question tentatively. Cynthia didn't hesitate. She was going to answer her way no matter what question was posed.

She looked toward the corner and back at Marcus, chagrin on her face. "She said you have to wait a bit for that answer."

Marcus decided to test the waters with his next question. *Leading the witness. But I have solid reasoning, ladies and gentlemen of the jury. Hear me out.*

"When your mom talks to you, do you feel at peace or is it

frightening?" Two options; close down the question. If she truly was answering her way, he would probably get an open response. That was his hope, at least.

Cynthia furrowed her brow and bit her bottom lip, thinking of the proper answer to the question. "I wouldn't say at peace. At first, I was scared. I didn't believe she was my mom. Then she told me something only she would have known, and I knew it was her. Talking to her still makes the hairs on my neck stand up tall, but I like talking to her. It's nice. And she protects me."

"From the other thing."

"Yeah. Mostly."

"What do you mean mostly?"

"Sometimes she knows things. She knew you were coming, and she said you were going to help us." Cynthia smiled a genuine kid smile at Marcus.

"I am going to do my best. Have you had any other encounters with the—"

"Dark man?" Cynthia interrupted him, but a flush of red went up her cheeks when she realized she had interrupted.

Marcus waved the thought away. "That wasn't rude. You're fine. You refer to him as the *Dark Man*? How come?"

Cynthia started to fidget, and Marcus could tell she was wholly uncomfortable talking about the *Dark Man*, but he needed to get as much information as he could in order to take the proper action.

It took her a long time to muster up the courage to say anything, and Marcus waited patiently. Finally, she glanced at the corner and then whispered, "Have you ever seen a shadow without a person?" Marcus said nothing, just waited. "He is like that. You can step through him, and you feel cold, but he isn't really there. Not unless you ask him to be there, and there is no way I would do that. Mom says it's too dangerous, especially for a kid."

Marcus was afraid that he was becoming numb to this palpable sense of dread. It was becoming a constant companion at this house. Every time it seemed that things were looking brighter, a new piece of information was presented that doused the wick.

This was the first moment he thought that maybe he wouldn't be taking this family's money. There was something bigger at stake here. But he couldn't stop yet.

"Why don't you like talking about him?"

Still whispering she said, "Because he listens. And gets mad. My daddy said that people who get really mad are friggin' pissed." She glanced over at the corner almost apologetically for saying the words. "Daddy said it."

"Do you know a secret of his? Is that why he's so...friggin' pissed?"

Cynthia tried to smile, but it fell off her lips almost before it arrived. Tears filled her eyes, and Marcus felt a slight breeze pass by him. He was certain now that it was Cynthia's mother. She didn't like seeing her daughter in distress and went to comfort her. Cynthia spoke through her emotion. "Yeah, I do. I know that he—"

Her words were cut off by a howling wind and banging on the back door of the garage. Cynthia didn't jump, but her whole body started shaking and the tears trickled out of her eyes, falling to the ground.

Marcus felt a wave of cold and if he had been newer to the profession, he would have assumed it was the spirit of the *Dark Man*, but he recognized it as a clear warning from Cynthia's mom. *Back off or the* Dark Man *will be the least of your concerns.*

He also was now sure that unless the *Dark Man* became powerfully desperate there was no way he would be able to break through the barrier of the garage, if he even knew how. But sometimes rage overwhelms knowledge, and that was when this little visit could suddenly turn exceedingly dangerous.

Marcus changed tactics to put Cynthia, and her mother, back at ease. "What's your mother's name?"

This snapped Cynthia back into the present and a smile appeared on her face even as she brushed back the tears. "Maria."

"That is a beautiful name. I had a sister named Maria. She died a long time ago."

"When she was my age," Cynthia said with complete confidence.

Marcus nodded his head. "That's right. Your mom just tell you that?"

"Uh huh. She also said we shouldn't talk about *you-know-who* anymore. Not until you are ready." Marcus found it a bit eerie to be talking to a dead woman through her daughter, but he *had* seen stranger things in his career.

"What should we talk about?" Marcus asked, crossing his left leg over his right knee. His back was starting to hurt, but he felt like there was still a lot left in this conversation.

"Do you like horses?" The question was so unexpected Marcus laughed out loud, and immediately saw he had hurt the girl's feelings. He held his hand up to show her it wasn't anything personal.

"I am not laughing at you, sweetie. It was just an unexpected question after talking about…what we were talking about. That's all. Please forgive me. I *do* like horses. In fact, I grew up on a ranch a couple hour drive from here, and we had at least fifteen horses at all times."

A wide smile broke onto Cynthia's face and she looked genuinely like a six-year-old for the first time since he met her.

"Me too. I always wanted one, but my parents could never afford it.

I always asked Santa, but then I found out he wasn't real. So, I stopped asking." Cynthia sighed, almost as if she were trying to manipulate the ghost of her mother into getting her a horse.

"Why do you ask?" Marcus was curious about the turn in topic.

"My mom said that you never learned to ride your horses. She says you would pet them when they were in their stalls, but never had the courage to ride one."

Cynthia looked shocked at this new information. "Really? You never rode one? What's wrong with you?" She blushed deeply again and stared off into space a moment before slapping a hand over her mouth so violently that he thought she may have given herself a bloody lip.

Marcus guessed that her mom had told her that it was because of a horse that his sister died. They had been out near the stables one day and three of the horses got spooked and ran out of the stable. A possum family had made a nest in the corner of one of the stalls and mama possum had nipped at the heels of the nearest horse, which set off a proximity panic. Marcus's dad tried to corral the horses and was having a difficult time of it.

Little Maria tried to help by going into the stable and attempting to calm down the other horses, which were skittish after the initial panic. She walked up to one of the horses making shushing sounds and patted it on its rear flank. The horse was still very spooked and immediately started bucking and kicking. Maria had no chance to get out of the stall. It took one kick and the horse caved in her skull, sending her beyond the earth.

The worst part of the whole situation was that it took nearly half an hour for anyone to find her. The confusion had been so great no one noticed she was missing. The horse broke a leg when it slammed into the wall of its stall, and when Marcus's father finally found Maria's broken body, he was filled with the irrational rage that anything dared hurt his daughter. He had a shotgun in the stable, grabbed it, put it flush against the horse's forehead and pulled the trigger.

His father had never been the same after that. He sold the ranch, moved to a small rural area and started the dreaded task of drinking himself to death. That is, until Marcus was born two years later.

"I never knew my sister. She died before I was born. I wasn't told the story of how she died until I was a teenager. I wasn't even told I had a sister. My dad died when I was eighteen. He drank himself to death. His liver failed. And from that moment on I was on my own." He smiled ruefully. "I haven't thought about that story in a long time."

"What happened to your mom?" Cynthia asked innocently. Marcus didn't think the question came from her mom.

"She died giving birth to me. It was me and my dad ever since I could remember. He did his best. I still miss him." Involuntary tears filled Marcus's eyes and he blinked them away quickly.

Cynthia stared off into the distance for a moment and then nodded her head. "My mom said she thinks you're ready."

"To know who the *Dark Man* is?" he whispered.

Cynthia nodded again. "And some other stuff. Stuff she doesn't want me to know."

Marcus looked at Cynthia, confused. "How is she going to tell me about these things without you knowing? I don't understand."

"She said this might be the hard part. She said that this is your moment. The moment you choose to help or walk away. And she wouldn't blame you if you walked away. But she has to ask you anyway."

Cynthia looked as though she had no idea what her mom was talking about, but a prickling sensation attached itself to the back of Marcus's head and a thought from somewhere outside his brain came to him: *This is where everything changes.*

"What does she need me to do?" Even as he asked the question, doubts arose in his mind. He wasn't sure if he wanted to hear an answer. Yes, he wanted to help this family, but at what cost to himself? *Was* there a cost that was too high? He thought about his father and the fight he put up to try and stay upright. A battle he lost. He didn't want to make such a choice, and he had a very sudden and desperate urge to run right out of the open garage door and never look back. Forget this family. He would deal with his troubled conscience later.

But, he already knew he wasn't going, not yet. He was curios. It edged its way inside his thoughts, and he knew if he didn't at least continue it would nag at him like an unreachable itch between his shoulder blades. So, instead of running, screaming into the afternoon sun he turned to Cynthia and smiled.

Cynthia took this as a sign that he was ready to listen. "My mom wants to know if she can speak to you directly."

"What does that mean?" He was stunned. And immediately an idea, but not one he wanted to entertain as real, scraped across his mind.

"She needs permission to come inside?" Cynthia looked at Marcus, hoping he would explain. "I don't know what that means."

He didn't explain, but he knew instantly what Maria was asking of him. She was requesting to come inside his mind and speak to him there. It was the thing he had always told himself he would never do. To do this would be to open himself up to her knowing all of him while she kept any information she wanted hidden, to herself. It was a one-sided deal, one that Marcus was certain he wouldn't take. In fact, he took pride in the fact that he had never invited an otherworld spirit inside. And now, to be deflowered right here and now for a family he had just met earlier the same day?

Marcus noticed that Cynthia's nose was scrunched up as if she smelled something off or was trying to understand something that was beyond her comprehension. "What is it?" he asked her.

"My mom said if you had any doubts, she could tell you more about your dream about the—" she searched for the word, "whirler devils? Something like that."

Marcus's stomach dropped into his feet. The bottom half of his body became very heavy and he thought he might sink through the chair into the earth and be buried alive. His mind reeled and his next thought was that he was going to vomit all over the garage floor.

Realizing he was hyperventilating, he focused his breathing, slowing it down until the world stopped spinning. Then he started to internally ask questions, questions he didn't dare ask aloud; at least not yet. *Was there more significance to the whirling dervish dream he had been having? How would she know about a dream? What else does she know?*

He took another few deep breaths and then focused on Cynthia. "Can you tell your mom that if she can guarantee she's not messing with me, we might be able to talk?"

Cynthia giggled. "Duh, she can hear you. And she said there is no real way for her to guarantee that she's not messing with you. But she says that you are a smart person and you know that she's not messing with you."

Marcus bit the inside of his cheek until he tasted the salty tang of copper on his tongue. This really would change everything if he allowed it to happen. He had no idea if he would be able to get her out of his head once she got inside. And there was always the story of the wolf in sheep's clothing, and something Biblical about demons shining false light. What if this was one of those instances? What if the entity that was talking to Cynthia was simply pretending to be her mom?

But what if it truly was her mom? He thought about the rush of air he had felt and had instinctively chocked it up to Cynthia's mom rushing over to protect her daughter. The decision was still a daunting one to make, but he felt the only other option he had at this point was to turn tail and run. And Marcus Grimm was a lot of things, but a coward wasn't on that list.

"Okay. Maria. I know you can hear me. How do we do this?" His legs started to shake in his nervousness.

Cynthia looked at Marcus. "She says you need to open your mind and give her permission to come inside. And she will do the rest."

Marcus nodded slightly, his nerves jangling around like wind chimes in a storm. "What is it going to feel like?"

Cynthia simply shrugged.

Marcus sat back in his chair and started his slow breathing again. He felt sort of silly, not knowing exactly how to 'invite' a spirit into his head. So, he simply thought *Maria, I give you permission to come inside my head. I open myself up to you.* And he waited, wincing at every sound that passed through the garage.

Although it felt like an eternity, only a few seconds later he felt fingers reach inside his head and squeeze his mind. He let out a silent scream and waited for death to come.

CHAPTER 5

This feeling was new to Marcus. The first sensation was that of fingers pressing against his skull, immediately followed by the impression of those fingers sinking through his skull and infiltrating his brain. This was accompanied by intense pain as if invisible appendages wove into his head and pulsated in his mind. It was an intrusion, an invasion, a penetration of his mental being. Though invited he resisted. It felt singularly unpleasant, taking from him without permission or boundary.

But then the pain morphed into pleasure as the fingers found old familiar places and incorporated themselves like an old friend syncing to the rhythm of camaraderie. The warm feeling, like the first hit of a good Scotch, dissolved into euphoric pleasure. He felt himself grow stiff and somewhere deep in his mind he hoped this was merely a mental feeling and not a physical one manifesting itself in the physical world. But it felt so real it became almost painful again; pain that needed a release to wrack his body with a climax that would destroy his world. And yet it remained, holding on, pushing to the extreme and then easing off, leaving him unfulfilled and lusting for more, almost demanding that the sensation take complete control.

He knew if that were to happen, he would scream, in pleasure and pain and the spectrum between. But it never happened. It held him in that suspended animation of near completion, and he thought for a moment *This must be what it is to gaze upon the face of God.* Unbearable, yet glorious. Perfection beyond human comprehension. And the other thought that came to him on its heels was that if he was allowed to finish, to reach the ecstasy, he would have nothing to say except *Thank you very much and a nice day to you too.*

There was another feeling mingling with everything else that made Marcus wonder if his body would be able to withstand this process much longer. Maybe his body would explode in a shower of light and particles and fluids, and maybe that would be all right.

It took him a moment to realize the new sense was falling; that feeling when one was near to sleep and the body jerked involuntarily. Panic set in, his rational mind telling him that if he fell too far, he would splatter on the ground like a peach dropped from a great height. His insides would become his outsides, and everyone would witness his demise like a grisly inkblot, nothing left to distinguish the mess of viscera as a human being.

And then as suddenly as it began, it stopped. Every bit of pain, every bit of pleasure, gone. He squeezed his eyes shut, not wanting to see what was happening, hoping for and dreading the cocktail of emotion to flood him again. But it did not come. His feet were on solid ground and he could hear someone stirring liquid with a spoon.

Hesitantly, he opened his eyes and found himself standing in a garden room with hanging plants surrounding him. There were ferns and succulents and herbs and what appeared to be drying leaves, perhaps tea. In the center of the room was a woman, sitting and rhythmically stirring her spoon in a dark liquid in her cup. Fine china. *So, this is where it went,* Marcus thought.

"Wondering where my fine china had run off to, Mr. Grimm?" The woman's voice was pure melody, pitch perfect, sounding more like singing than talking in its clarity.

"Something like that," Marcus croaked before clearing his throat.

The woman gestured at the seat across from her at the table. "Come and sit. Have tea with me."

Marcus hesitated, waiting for something to come out of a dark corner and...do what...he wasn't sure, but nothing pleasant. But there *were* no dark corners in this room; everything was well lit. He made his way to the table. The chair squealed a high metallic scrape as he pulled it away from the table and when he sat, he found it quite comfortable. Everything seemed and felt so...real, so...there. How could this possibly be happening, sitting here while his physical body was sitting, lifeless perhaps, in a chair elsewhere?

"Our brains are incredibly powerful, Mr. Grimm. Everything we perceive – touch, taste, smell, see – is accumulated and processed through our minds to make it all real to us. Everyone perceives the universe in a slightly different way, because our brains are uniquely wired. What might be dark red to one person takes on a purplish hue to another. But they both call it the same color, even though they know it slightly differently. A singer may sound beautifully in tune to one person and horribly sharp to another. Our brains can also be terribly destructive as well because the rational tells us that what we imagine but do not see evidenced before our eyes, must be false. Imagination dies slowly as we age, and that is one of the greatest tragedies of humanity that I have witnessed." The woman paused to take a deep breath. Marcus found he couldn't speak and realized he was holding his breath. He exhaled in unison with the woman and felt himself start to relax. When she looked at him, he saw a glint in her eye.

"And to answer your other question, no one is going to see your…manifestation of lust back in the physical world. It's simply a mental expression of your brain trying to decode all the information it was given while you crossed."

Marcus felt color creep up his neck and his face became uncomfortably hot. He didn't know how to proceed, so he asked the simplest question to try and gain a little footing in this otherworld. "Are you Maria?"

"Very good, Mr. Grimm. I knew you would get there." Her tone wasn't condescending, but simply affirmed his suspicions.

Marcus was surprised how quickly a sense of affection was growing for her, and easily understood what it was that John had seen in her. "How much do you know about me?"

Maria shrugged and sipped her tea. "You really should have some tea. I dry all the ingredients and make it fresh every day with spring water from the brook behind the house. This is a particularly potent Oolong that lingers on the tongue for long moments."

Marcus looked around again and found that he could hear the soft susurrus of the stream. "What is this place?"

"We will get to that," Maria responded. "But first, I need to tell you a few things."

Marcus nodded his head and leaned forward. He found that he wanted to know everything Maria did. And he wanted to sit and listen to her forever.

"You are Marcus Samuel Grimm, born 1976 to Samantha and Matthias Grimm. Their second child of three. You discovered early that you had an ability, let's call it a sensitivity, to the otherworld.

Instead of becoming a two-bit charlatan you chose to use this gift to help people. You make enough money to live comfortably, but even if you didn't you would still be in the same line of work. Family is long gone, so you have no real ties on Earth, which makes your job easier. Although you drink moderately, you don't drink to forget what you've seen or have done. Am I near it?"

"On top of it, more like," he acknowledged. "That's probably what my obituary will say. However, one small correction. My mother died in childbirth, so I was the second child of two."

Marcus hoped he didn't sound disrespectful. He was also relieved that she had gotten at least one detail wrong.

"Okay," she responded and smiled. But her tone was that of someone who knew details he didn't and was obliging him for the time being, and this was a bit unnerving.

"I am Maria Sarah Caldwell Chambers. I was born in 1985 to Javier and Marianna Juarez. I was an only child, and lived an ordinary life. I met John as he was finishing college and I a bright-eyed freshman. We dated for five years before he asked me to marry him. It took us three miscarriages to finally have one stick, my sweet Cynthia. Two years after that we welcomed Charlie into the world, and three years later I was diagnosed with cancer. Now, here we are, as old friends." Maria smiled again and this time Marcus smiled back.

"I'm now going to tell you a little about this otherworld, and hopefully by the end of it you will be willing and able to help me. Please do not interrupt me, because time is short. And it will be even shorter once *he* figures out what is happening."

She paused to make sure Marcus understood what she was saying. He opened his mouth to ask who *he* was but thought better of it and simply nodded. He already knew.

"When you die you don't see lights. You don't stand before an almighty God who judges your entire life as you stand before Him. At least, not right away. There *are* spirits that roam the Earth; lost souls who either couldn't or chose not to pass through to the eternal. Among that group are three types: The first type are the ones that are angry. They didn't deserve to die, so they decide they shouldn't be dead. These are often what people refer to as poltergeists; enraged and entitled humans who believe they got the sharp end of the stick in life. Their anger is unbelievably powerful and has the most influence on the physical world. They can move things, manipulate items, even in rare situations, violate people. You have encountered some of this type.

"Second are the confused ones. These are the spirits that are not able to find their way to the eternal. And it's not typically people who suffered from Alzheimer's, death clears that right up, or myriad other brain inflictions. These spirits are the ones who never truly knew themselves. They went through life jumping from one thing to the next in search of purpose and meaning outside of their innate being. Finding your identity outside of your own self is one of the most dangerous pursuits not just for life, but for afterlife. Again, I'm not talking about people with depression or mental illness. You know those people who must make it known to as many people as possible where they stand? The 'I'm Vegan, I'm into CrossFit, my spiritual journey took me to this Ashram where they usually don't allow photos, but they could sense my inner purity and allowed me to take pictures' type of crap. It's the equivalent of getting people to jerk off your ego. Those are the people who are confused when they die, because they never truly knew who they were.

"I am in the third subset. I *chose* to stay behind. Before I died, I felt the presence of something in our house. A malevolent force that wanted to destroy my family. Instead of fully crossing over, I decided to stay behind to protect my family.

"And yes, I know the question you are internally asking, Mr. Grimm. No, once I have fulfilled my task I don't get to go to the eternal. That's the biggest load of horse manure that I had to learn the hard way. You can't help a spirit settle their last debt or reconcile with a loved one and send them forth into the hold-me-tight-light of eternity. I am a doomed soul, but I made that decision, unless..." she paused almost wistfully and then returned with resolve. "But, I chose to protect my family. Ain't no pity for the devil or a soul who chooses their own destiny.

"My family is in danger, my children in particular. This is the only reason I chose this extreme. And you, Mr. Grimm, must be a willing participant every step of the way or this doesn't work. This is why I brought you here and why I have a few things to show you before you return to your physical body. I'm not going to lie and say this will be easy or safe. It won't. But you are the only one I have found that even comes close to the capability I need to pull this off."

Marcus waited a few seconds to make sure she was done, and then he spoke in a hushed tone. "Uh huh," was all he could manage at first. "Uh, Marcus. Please call me Marcus."

She let him recover in silence. And then he spoke, "Uh, wow! That's a lot. I never thought of someone choosing to remain. That is heartbreaking." He took a deep breath and continued, "You sensed that I would be able to help when I came into your house?"

Maria shook her head. "I sensed you out in the world. *I* brought you to my house so we could have this conversation."

She could tell by the look on his face that he wasn't really understanding, but again allowed him time to think it through until he came to the conclusion himself. A lightbulb moment.

"You influenced John. You got him to hire me."

"It was easy once Cynthia was on board. Poor Charlie is already starting to cave in on himself, because of that other bastard." Her eyes flared with anger. "His influence is already strong. I know you are going to talk to Charlie, and I wish I could be there for that, but *he*..." When she said '*he*' she spat the word out with venom. "*He* won't let me into the room. I can catch glimpses, but if *he* knows I am there *he* forces me away."

Marcus thought about the situation for a long while, and again Maria let him. She sipped her tea, got up and tended to a couple plants, spritzing them with water, and grabbed a box from a cabinet Marcus hadn't noticed before. *She probably kept me from noticing until now.* By the time she sat back down at the table, Marcus had made up his mind.

"I am considering helping you. But I have a few questions first." Marcus had learned in his short time with this woman that a direct approach was the best.

Maria chuckled. "Let's not get ahead of ourselves. You don't even know what it is that I need from you. I *am* glad you have a few questions. I would have made the wrong choice by sending for you if you didn't." Maria smiled her sweet smile and set the box on the table in front of her.

"What is this place?" Marcus felt like easing into the inquiry more for his sake than hers.

"I learned how to construct a place of solace for myself. It's not the eternal by any stretch, but it does fine in a pinch." She looked around her home away from home, admiring all the work she had put into it.

Another light clicked on in Marcus's head. "That's why you created a safe space in the garage. The kids go out to paint or color and you know they are safe enough there for you to come here for a while."

Maria put a finger to her nose. "Bingo. See, I told Cynthia you were smart."

But another, potentially urgent question occurred to him. "If we are here, aren't you concerned for Charlie? He was still in the house."

Maria's visage darkened considerably, reminding him of Gandalf when he admonished Frodo for questioning him. *I am not a conjurer of cheap tricks.*

"I am always concerned for my children. Don't be dense. Time moves differently here. That is one thing movies tend to get correct. Being tied to the flow of time on Earth means there are limitations to the difference, but to put it in perspective, you left your physical body about fifteen seconds ago."

The look of shock on Marcus's face caused the darkness to lift from Maria's face. "Wild, right? The eternal operates on an entirely separate timeframe. Eternity is always here and always now. The fact that we are tethered to Earth simply makes time move as through thick molasses. So, while I *am* adamantly concerned for my children, Marcus, the risk of this time away will all be worth it once you understand a little more and return to the physical world. Knowledge is powerful."

"So, what do you need me to do?" Even as the question left Marcus's lips the feeling of dread invaded. He suddenly felt exhausted. If the whirlwind he had already experienced wasn't enough, he knew that once he made his decision to help, everything would change. Forever.

"I need to send you to three places. Let's call the first one a history lesson. The second one is much more personal to you. And the third, the most dangerous, will clue you into a lot of the happenings in my house." Even Maria looked frightened when she mentioned the third place.

"So, not much then?" Marcus tried to make the question sound jokey, but it came out as a strangled hope that she had misspoken.

"There are some things that you will not be able to accept until you experience them for yourself. I will give you the groundwork, but you must do the digging." Slowly, Maria pushed the box in front of her across the table. "In here is a token for your first trip. It will help give you clarity."

Marcus gulped. "Really?"

"Sure. I don't know. Consider it a placebo. Placebos work psychologically. Just allow it to be psychological or whatever."

Maria threw her hands in the air. "Blue pill; red pill; box token. Clap your hands if you believe in fairies. I don't really care; you just have to be fully willing to let me work my magic. I'm not a conjurer of cheap tricks." Marcus raised an eyebrow.

"Yeah, I got that from you. Now steady up, ready up, and pucker up. You're going on a ride, Alice."

Marcus touched the box and ran his hand along the wood. The wood was smooth and crafted with great care. He felt the hinges and then ran his thumb over the latch.

"Enough of the foreplay, Casanova. Get in there already."

Marcus opened the lid, which creaked satisfyingly on its hinges.

"Oh, and in case you were wondering, this isn't going to be nearly the mind melt it was to get you here. It'll be more like sliding sideways." Maria gestured to the box impatiently.

Marcus reached inside and pulled out a small demon chess piece. His brow furrowed and he looked up at Maria. "What the hell is—" Before he could finish the question, he felt himself slip. Then the world went dark.

CHAPTER 6

The first sensation was a sudden, gut-wrenching stop. The slide ended abruptly, turning his stomach into a sea of turmoil. Saliva rushed into his mouth and the desire to vomit was strong. He kept his eyes closed, trying to orient his stomach in the proper position and felt the nausea slowly abate.

The second sensation was of being in a dank tunnel with torches lining the walls. There was a scraping sound, low and deliberate, like something was being dragged against cobblestone.

Marcus opened one eye, his vision adjusting instantaneously. His other eye followed soon after, showing him that indeed, he *was* in a tunnel, such as one might find in Victorian Era London. The stones surrounding him were dotted with moss, and an occasional weed sprouted between the masonry. He took a breath, smelling the slightly salty air mixed with the cloyingly musky odor of dampness. The odor was moldy, like an old house in disrepair.

He looked around for the dragging sound and saw two men walking briskly toward him. One was dragging a tarpaulin and the other, older and grey, held a Bible in a white-knuckled grasp with a rosary draped over one hand and a vial in the other. They continued to make their way straight at Marcus, and when he realized there was no place for him to dodge, he instinctively threw his hands out in front of his face to stop them from running him over.

A moment later the two men dissolved through him and continued on their way, leaving Marcus looking at his hands.

The younger one dragging the tarp said, "Father Munroe, I do wish thee to be a bit more concerned by the lateness of the hour."

At first the words sounded like gibberish, but when they traveled into Marcus's ears it was as if a translator was giving him the contemporary parallel of what was being spoken. Marcus assumed they were speaking Olde English and surmised he was in England sometime in the 1800s.

Father Munroe turned sharply toward the man with the tarp. He was angry, but Marcus could also see a ring of fear circling his eyes. "Francis, if we do not attend to this man now, we may lose him eternally!" Father Munroe turned and stalked off down the tunnel. Francis stared after him and after some deliberation decided to continue to follow.

"I am simply stating the Whitechapel M-"

Father Munroe turned on his heel and this time his face came within inches of Francis's. He was clearly enraged, but Marcus still had no idea what any of this meant; where he was, why he was here, or who these people were.

"This murderer thou speakest of, is nothing more than a common street child of a whore. He is a lowly inbreed who cannot keep his manhood in his trousers, so he atones for the lack of self-control by murdering street walkers. We have nothing to fear."

Father Munroe bumped his chest against Francis at this point.

Francis tried to stand his ground but stumbled a step back. "Do thee fancy thyself a street walker? Are thou fearful of evisceration?"

Francis shook his head slowly. "I am simply stating that I am frightened of the prospect of wandering within his circle, lest he decide a desire for other victims be prudent."

Father Munroe thumped Francis on the head with the Bible. "Have thee no faith, cur? Thou travelest with a man of faith, yet thee doubt and quail in fear. Thy movements rise to the surface for all to smell, Francis. Gird thine loins and come. A man is in need this eve and *I'll* be damned if I allow *him* to be damned."

Francis rubbed his forehead a moment, and it was then that Marcus could see just how young he was, no more than a teenager. Father Munroe continued and Francis reluctantly followed, muttering something about *do what Father says* under his breath, and Marcus wondered if he was actually Munroe's son. Then he remembered that Priests had to take a vow of celibacy and put the thought out of his head.

Marcus continued to take in his surroundings as he walked behind the two men. The tunnel twisted and turned and seemed endless until they abruptly surfaced on a street in front of a dark house. Immediately, Marcus felt the chill in the air. He was reminded of the movie poster for *The Exorcist* and involuntarily shivered. Father Munroe and Francis stopped for a moment, eyeing the house as if they were trying to determine the best insertion point during a military operation.

Father Munroe pointed at the house and looked at Francis. "Once we enter that house there will be no turning back. Thou must remain strong and show no signs of fear. The work we do here tonight is desperate and must be accomplished with haste. Are thee prepared for this, my son?"

Francis swallowed hard and Marcus could hear the click in the kid's throat as he did. For a long time, Father Munroe and Francis stared at each other, like they were playing a game of mental chicken, waiting for the other to say, "Screw it, let's go home and get drunk. That's sounds like a better plan."

After what felt like an eternity, Francis simply nodded his head. As Father Munroe moved across the street, Francis reached out for him but missed. Marcus could see the intensity of the fear in the lad's eyes and felt pity for the boy. If they *were* headed into an exorcism, and if it *was* anything like Hollywood typically portrayed them, this poor young man was going to be scarred for life. Marcus had a flash of Francis taking up the mantle of Jack the Ripper and continuing his work, but with people who had offended God's sensibility, instead of hookers.

The three of them entered the house, two unaware of the one, and were met by a feeble looking old man who was wringing his hands in a mechanical motion that suggested it was subconscious. "Thank God thou hast arrived. He is bad off. In the basement. We had to rope him to the wall. It took four of us to subdue him."

Father Munroe, who had himself looked frightened on the street, stared into the old man's eyes with confidence and resolve and said, "We will do what we are able, yet I can promise thee nothing. These are delicate dealings, and on occasion the host has refused to relinquish the parasite. I do not wish to frighten thee, but I must inform thee of the truth before we begin."

The old man nodded, and tears filled his eyes, one drop tracing its way down his face. "I understand thee very well. Now, please, follow me."

The troupe marched down a set of old wooden stairs that groaned as if they were going to collapse at any moment. As soon as they cleared the landing the group gagged and gasped for air. The smell in the room was of rotten flesh. It was putrid and made Marcus think the stink was somehow gangrenous. He could taste the putrescence and it brought his gorge to the top of his throat once again, but, as before, he held the contents at bay.

For the first time, he wondered about the limitations of this 'vision' in which no one could see or hear him, but he could smell the vileness in the air. He figured there was a purpose behind the contradiction, and then let it pass from his mind.

Just as Marcus re-gained his mental footing, he heard the low growl. It sounded like a pit bull trained to attack on sight. There was nothing human in the sound and for a moment Marcus felt intense fear paralyze him. His breathing and heartrate grew rapid and he was hyperventilating. He didn't know and didn't want to find out if he could pass out in this fever dream, so he leaned over his knees and took in deep breaths through his nose and exhaled through his mouth in an explosive, silent whistle.

While the stench of the room was muted by his desperation to stay upright, he was aware he was sucking this diseased air into his lungs with great gusto. Hopefully, whatever contamination he was breathing wouldn't affect his physical body.

I got lung cancer by traveling to Victorian England in my incorporeal body and breathing in the black plague through my nose. Thank you very much and a nice day to you too.

Marcus continued to follow the others and rounding a corner saw a man, a loose term at this point, with ropes around his wrists and ankles splayed against the wall wearing nothing but the filthy remains of a nightgown. The gaunt contours of his emaciated body were accentuated by the sheerness of the clothing. It appeared as if the man had hardly eaten in weeks.

Marcus could count his ribs and the man's skin was so translucent, his internal organs were almost visible. His eyes were closed, and he was breathing rapidly. Marcus wondered if the man could endure an exorcism. Even if they were able to remove the demon would he have the strength to get up survive the ordeal? Did these people have any idea what they were doing? Another wave of palpable fear rose in him.

The group stopped in front of the man, keeping a good ten feet between them and the supposedly possessed. Spread against the wall, the man seemed to take little notice, until a smile grew on his face, even before he opened his eyes. It was not a happy smile, but twisted and sinister. It felt as if he had just seen inside the soul of every other person in the room, numbering six, besides Marcus, and found them all lacking. Without looking up the growl in the man's throat grew and he murmured a string of nonsensical words. Even the translator buried in Marcus's psyche could not decipher them.

Father Munroe stepped forward and held the cross out in front of his face. "Whatever spirit resides within this man; I command thee out. Out in the name of the Father and the Son and the Holy Ghost. Thou hast no place within this vessel. Thou layest no claim to this child of God."

His hands began to tremble ever so slightly and the man against the wall lifted his head and cackled. It sounded like dry leaves crunched beneath a boot heel, and it was decidedly hostile. Marcus felt the physical and spiritual shift of power in the room. There was no way this would end well. The power the demon already commanded in the room was enough to make it hard to breathe, as if there was an added weight to the atmosphere. Marcus began to feel drowsy and remembered this was how demons took what they wanted. Allow a demon to exist in this plane without consequences for long and they could dull even the sharpest minds. He didn't understand how he knew this to be true, but it was as apparent to him as the answer of two plus two.

He scanned the room and could see the effect it was having on the others; the four men who had tied the man-demon to the wall seemed as if they were unable to keep their eyes open. One of them went completely slack-jawed and hit the ground with a sickening crunch as his skull connected with the cobblestones. A small rivulet of blood wound its way around the cobbles and the man started to convulse; a brain injury. The victim was gone before anyone had a chance to move and help him.

Father Munroe remained perfectly still with his eyes closed, which tick-tocked behind the lids like a manic clock. Francis vomited. Marcus started his deep breathing exercises. It felt as if the only thing that remained in the room was the possessed man against the wall. He was growing to fill up the entire space, pushing everything else out. No room in the inn.

Father Munroe opened his eyes and Marcus saw an incredible determination in the man's eyes that gave Marcus hope that perhaps this would not end as poorly as anticipated.

Father Munroe opened his mouth and uttered a single phrase that caused the world to drop out from beneath Marcus's feet. "I command thee to remove thyself from the body of Garrett Grimm immediately."

As the name entered Marcus's ears his whole body went numb. He tried to process what he heard, but it seemed the translator had taken time off.

The name had been spoken, but it didn't seem possible to Marcus;

there had to be a mistake.

Yet, he knew it was no mistake. This was why he had been sent to this event.

Scrambling, he quickly did the math in his head and settled on great-great-grandfather. His ancestry had a history of possession. This introduced a whole host of questions that buzzed through his mind like angry hornets. Is this why I have my abilities? Is it a genetic thing? Did possession alter the DNA of the person, so something from outside became inherent and was passed down the generations? These questions came fast and hard and Marcus thumped heavily to the ground, his mind reeling.

The man-demon smiled his sickly smile and looked directly at Father Munroe. "Father, thou hast no authority over me. Thou can't claim power when thou hast been stripped of them."

Francis looked at Father Munroe with a wary look but held his tongue. Father Munroe continued to stare the man-demon in the eyes; not so much as a flicker of concern shot through his eyes. He looked like a man of authority.

Marcus looked up from where he now sat on the dirt floor and saw Father Munroe physically dig in his heels, as if he were preparing to be shoved by this creature. He took a deep breath, steeled himself and said, "I have all the authority of Jesus the Christ, our Lord. And I command thee to release this man from your unholy grasp. The power of Christ outshines thine power tenfold and shan't be denied."

He took a step toward the man-demon and it appeared to Marcus as if it took great effort. "What is thy name, demon?"

Instead of answering Father Munroe, the man-demon turned his gaze on Francis. A grisly smile crossed its face that sent chills down Marcus's spine. "This is thy bastard, yes? Thou hast committed a cardinal sin against your *god*," the man-demon spit the word out as if it were acid on its tongue. "So how can thou sayest thee hath authority over me?"

Francis's face went white as a sheet, giving the man-demon the only answer he needed on the subject. It smiled again and dark brown grime seeped between its teeth, some spilling out and dribbling down its chin. "Thou art the bastard. Son of a whoremonger. Son of a bitch mother. Why art thou here? Thou hast no authority over me either."

The words seemed to have struck Francis dumb. His mouth worked up and down as he tried to respond, and when Marcus looked over at his father he knew the man was praying his son would not be able to find words.

But he finally did find his voice, and when he spoke, Francis spoke clearly and with great authority. "Verily, I *am* the bastard son of Munroe. Son of a whoremonger and a bitch mother. That means I know myself. Thou dost not proclaim any surprise of character. Dost thou know thyself? I think thou hast not an idea. Thou art commanded by the unholiest host to torture and destroy, but thou hast no authority. Thou art a vazey ratbag with the spine of a jellyfish. I know who I am; who art thou?"

The fire in Francis's eyes grew as he spoke, and Marcus saw a glimmer of hope as the outburst concluded.

Marcus had no idea what a *vazey ratbag* was but judging by the looks of the others in the room it was quite the insult. In Marcus's head he figured Francis had just called the man-demon a name that was a bit worse than simply saying he was a scumbag. This brought a slight smile to his face and he found himself respecting and trusting the boy's presence in this dark place. This boy had thrown the twisted words of the demon back at him, nullifying its power.

It took Marcus a moment to realize something was off, but when he looked up it was evident that the man-demon was staring directly at him. He shifted to one side and its eyes followed. An unsettling feeling worked its way into Marcus's chest. Surely this demon could not see him. This was a vision; a dream; a spiritual awakening. Once more he moved, and again the demon's eyes followed him.

"And who do we have here?" The man-demon spoke in Marcus's common vernacular. All the men turned and looked toward Marcus. For a moment Marcus thought they must all see him, but their eyes shifted around and through him, trying to figure out to whom the demon was speaking.

Marcus remained silent, hoping the attention would shift back to the physically present and just when it seemed like it might the demon spoke again. "I asked you who you were, vagrant. You don't belong here. This is not your place."

A thought went through the demon's head. "This isn't even your time. Tell me who you are!" Marcus felt the demon's demand in his chest and he instinctively took a step back. The man physically lifted away from the wall, pulling his restraints taut.

"Who I am is no concern of yours. These men want to know your name. Tell them your name. Give them what they want." The men in the room looked at each other, confused at what was occurring.

"What new devilry is this?" Father Munroe asked to the air in the room.

"Stay out of this, Father. This does not concern thee." The demon turned back to Marcus, moving its vessel's left eye first and then the right until its full attention and intention rested back on him. "Tell me your name and I will tell you mine."

Marcus laughed. Before he knew he was going to laugh it squeezed out through his teeth. Somehow the demon speaking in a modern tongue made it lose some of its power over him. "Like I'm going to trust a demon to follow through on that deal."

The demon pulled against the ropes again, testing their strength. "Then you don't get mine. Quid pro quo."

Marcus looked around the room. Obviously, the others were at a complete loss. They didn't know what to do and shifted restlessly from one foot to the other, listening to one side of a conversation in a form of English they couldn't understand. This made Marcus grin, which in turn infuriated the demon.

"What's so funny?" the demon demanded. "I could destroy you."

"I mean, you certainly could try." Marcus's confidence was growing exponentially.

The demon slumped against the wall for a moment. Marcus felt a small nudge in his mind and deeper in his soul. If the demon was trying to conjure unsavory evidence which he could use to gain the upper ground, Marcus was certain it wouldn't find anything worth mentioning. But the demon surprised him.

"You are Grimm's twice great grandson. Your father is Mathias and your mother is Samantha." The blood ran out of Marcus's face and the demon saw its opening. "You have power, but it's not natural. It was given to you. It was gifted to you."

For a moment Marcus thought he saw a flicker of fear pass through the demon's eyes. "Why are you here? What do you want with me?"

"I want your name," Marcus replied, hoping the demon wouldn't sense that he had no idea either, besides the obvious lineage connection.

"And if I give you my name, you will leave?" The demon looked skeptical.

Marcus tried to not hesitate for too long in his reply, hoping the demon would believe his words were true. "Yes." A simple, satisfying response.

"Lies." The demon spat back immediately.

"Truth." The lie wasn't very convincing, and Marcus knew it. He could have spotted the lie before it was out of his mouth, so of course a demon had no problem.

The body on the wall relaxed and the demon clucked its tongue. "You *are* lying, but I am intrigued by you. I will tell you my name, but I don't believe it will serve any meaning for you."

Marcus shrugged his shoulders and thought to himself that this is not nearly as nasty a proceeding as he thought it was going to be. He was sure that normally the exorcism process in the 1800s was much more intense and draining, but Marcus had created a wrinkle that stopped the proceedings, at least for the moment. And he had the demon's attention. He hoped Father Munroe would be able to see an opportunity to strike while the demon was distracted.

"My name is Andromalius," the demon finally said. Father Munroe gasped and riffled through his Bible to find a particular passage. Francis looked frightened again but was holding it together very well. The name didn't mean anything to Marcus, but he held onto that bit of information while continuing to distract the demon.

"Andromalius? And what job do you have in hell?" Marcus hoped his tone sounded condescending, and when Andromalius responded, he knew he had succeeded.

Andromalius drew himself up on the wall, Garrett's feet lifting off the ground momentarily. "I command thirty-six legions of demons. I punish thieves and the wicked. I am a most powerful demon."

As Andromalius continued its speech, Marcus tried to think toward

Father Munroe. *Now! Now is your chance to exorcise this demon! Do not waste your opportunity!* But Father Munroe continued to search in his Bible.

Finally, Andromalius finished talking about all it did in the bowels of the netherworld and Marcus turned his attention back, whistling low in appreciation of all his accolades. This seemed to make the demon even angrier, and Garrett's body moved out from the wall into open space, trying to get to where Marcus sat. The fury in Andromalius's eyes burned into Marcus, again leaving him tired. Suddenly he wanted to simply close his eyes and sleep. He fought the feeling.

"You dare attempt to subvert my authority, you little pile of rat bones?" Andromalius's full and undivided attention was now on Marcus and Marcus started to pray in earnest for Father Munroe to take a damned hint.

"For your lack of respect, I will destroy every man in this room. I will condemn them all to an eternity in hell. Their blood will boil, their souls will turn to ash, and they will be tortured forever. Because of you!"

Garrett's body relaxed against the wall, and then with seemingly very little effort, Andromalius snapped the ropes holding the body to the wall. Marcus had not realized that Father Munroe had been muttering some sort of incantation from the Bible, but he seemed to be nearly finished with the words.

Fortunately, Andromalius had been so intent on his curiosity with the invisible stranger that it had not realized the words mumbled through Father Munroe's slightly parted lips either. And now it was too late.

Andromalius tried to regain its composure and focus on Father Munroe, but something was already happening. Water was being sprinkled on Andromalius, and Andromalius was screaming, and

Father Munroe finished with, "By the power of Jesus Christ, with all authority from the God of the heavens and the earth, and with the guidance of the Holy Spirit who commands authority over all, I compel thee damned demon to leave this man's body. I compel thee to be cast back into the fires of hell never to return to the earthly plain."

There was an ear-shattering scream that sounded like a rusty nail being drawn across a chalkboard. Everyone covered their ears, including Marcus. And then Garrett's body went completely limp and an old man emerged from his body holding a serpent. Andromalius was enraged and focused entirely on Marcus. "This is your fault! You invader! You intestinal cyst!" Andromalius charged across the room toward Marcus who was scooting backward on the floor. As Andromalius leaped, Marcus raised his hands in front of his face, doubting anything could *actually* stop the demon. In that instant, he felt the sliding sensation and knew he had escaped.

CHAPTER 7

Marcus re-emerged in the garden room, sitting at the table, still holding the demon token. As soon as he could think clearly, he dropped the demon token to the ground. Maria still sat in her seat, and looked at him, smiling. "Quite a rush, right?"

At first he couldn't find his voice, but then his eyes narrowed, and he pointed an accusatory finger at Maria. "That demon knew I was there. It knew I was in the room."

Maria sighed. "I know. There was a chance he wouldn't have noticed you, but as I've said before, the spiritual realm does not operate the same as the physical world. Time is different; existence is different. And it will do you no good to point your finger at me. So, put it away."

Marcus hadn't realized he was still pointing at Maria, so he lowered his hand to his lap.

"It came for me. It tried to get me. And it knew my history. It knew where I came from and said something about how my power was gifted to me. What does that even mean?" Before Maria could answer he asked the other question that was bothering him, "And how could I smell what was going on in that room? In the tunnel?"

Maria shrugged, which sent a new twinge of anger up Marcus's back. "I don't know. I have limited information." Her eyes shifted to another spot in the room, and Marcus realized she was lying to him.

He had learned to tell when people were lying and apparently it still worked, even with dead people. There were subconscious tics that one developed when trying to elude the truth.

The whole *a person blinks or looks up and to the left when they're lying* concept was simply a way for the experts to watch for a conscious attempt to not commit those tells. The truth was everyone had a different tell. One person might look up and to the left when telling a lie, but someone else might simply be attempting to remember something. There may be no deception in their retelling of an event.

People got nervous when they were being interrogated, which is why lie detectors were so inconsistent. It's the same with white coat syndrome; before a person walks into a doctor's office their blood pressure may be perfectly normal, but as soon as the nurse straps on that cuff and starts pumping the bulb, anxiety hits and they get a false reading of one fifty eight over one-o-seven.

Every single person reacts differently, so the only true way to tell if someone is lying is to spend a good deal of time watching how they answer questions they are asked; specifically, the reaction when they are asked the same question multiple times. Repetition more often than not rats out the liars.

It's the same when an expert is attempting to determine if someone is committing fraud with a signature. If the signature is exactly the same every time—the swoop is perfect on a letter, the crossing of the letters is similarly perfect, the expert knows it is fraud. Humans get fatigued, they aren't thinking about their signature, or they are thinking too much about their signature, so the swoops and crossings change and shift. The basic idea of the signature remains, but there is a level of degradation that proves its authenticity.

Then again, there were people who quite simply were terrible liars. Marcus didn't believe Maria was one of those people, but he knew her last statement was as untrue as a politician's promise. He decided not to push the issue, but tucked it in the back of his mind for a time it might be helpful.

Marcus was brought back from his reverie by Maria's hand being placed on his. "You have a very analytical mind, and a lot of this information you have to experience for yourself. If you don't *see* it with your own eyes, you have the ability to write it off in your head." Maria pointed to her head. "It becomes fantastical and wholly unreal." She tapped her breastbone. "But you need to believe it in your heart, or all of this is for naught."

Before he knew what was happening, Marcus found himself giggling. Maria's patient eyes simply looked at him, waiting for the reveal. "You sound like a Hallmark card."

Maria smiled, patted Marcus's hand one last time, leaned back in her chair, and said, "Well, I did enjoy a good birthday card." At this, they both laughed and for a brief moment, it felt as if the direness of the situation disappeared and each could catch their breath.

The laughter soon died down to a trickle and again a somber pall washed over the room. Maria looked at Marcus with concern in her eyes.

"You have two places left to visit, Scrooge. The first one was a cake walk compared to what you are about to go through." She held up a hand when Marcus opened his mouth. "And before you go asking me for more information you know I won't give you, here is what I will say: You need to keep an open mind on the second leg and a closed mind on the third. You will understand when you experience it for yourself."

"You really are infuriating, you know that." It was more of a statement than a question.

"Just wait until all this ends. Then you will truly know how infuriating I can be." Maria smiled and sipped her tea. "Any other questions I won't answer for you before you head off on your next adventure?"

Marcus took a deep breath and looked at the box that still sat in front of him. "Did you know the man who was being exorcised was my double great grandfather?"

"I did. There is a history in your family regarding demons and the otherworld. This is why I wanted you to be here to help me. I know you are still not convinced enough to lend your assistance, but hopefully once your journeys are complete you will agree to my request. Everything hinges on your acceptance." Maria suddenly looked very tired, and a little afraid. She truly was not convinced if Marcus would help her in the end.

He tried to lighten the mood. "I guess you could tell me there is no free will and that it is my fate, my destiny, to help you."

"I could. But you would tell me to cut the crap and find a short pier to take a long walk on. And that won't do anyone any good." Maria shrugged and closed her eyes. "I guess you still *could* do that anyhow, but I'm hoping that being as open and honest as I am able will give you more resolve to see this through."

Marcus nibbled on his lip, thinking about the ramifications of what she was saying. The implication was that if he helped her something big was going to occur. And that involved him, possibly in a life-altering way. He figured he was already chest deep, so he might as well see the other two experiences to the end. He could then decide what he was willing to do, based on whatever information he could gain. He needed to be clinical about it. The more emotion he allowed to seep into his decision, the more likely he was to make no consideration for himself in the end.

His fingers reached out and touched the box. The next token rested in there, and he was both curious and slightly terrified. His secret fear had always been confined spaces. If he pulled out a little coffin token, he was fairly certain he would call the whole thing off right then. But he knew he had to see the token. His palms started to sweat, and he exhaled slowly. "Okay. I think it's time to see what's in the box. And I swear to God, if it's Gwyneth Paltrow's head I am going to freak out." He forced a laugh out between his teeth, but there was no comedy in it.

Maria didn't smile. It seemed as though she had heard the joke a million times, and she probably had. People tended to run that sort of bit into the ground, through the mantle and into the core before they would let it go. He wasn't upset that she didn't care for his humor; he simply was hoping she would at least pretend.

"Remember, you will need to open your mind for this next trip. Sorry I don't have any mushrooms or anything to make the trip more psychedelic. They should be popping up sometime next spring."

Marcus couldn't tell if she was joking or not, so he didn't react. And then she added, "And don't worry, your...situation only lasted a couple minutes the last time you slid."

Marcus instantly felt heat rise into his face, and his mouth worked up and down silently. And then Maria was laughing. "I'm joking. Lighten up. You were fully slumped." Her tone changed abruptly. "So, relax and open the box. We're running out of time."

It took Marcus a moment to compose himself, and then he felt his fingers slide under the slight lip on the box, and when his fingernails found purchase, he lifted the lid, quietly and reverently. His hand found its way inside and wrapped around something with uneven dimensions. He pulled it out and looked at it, uncomprehending for a few seconds. His last thought before he slid was, *what does a dancing figurine have to do with anything.*

CHAPTER 8

Marcus opened his eyes and was staring at the ceiling. It was a very ornate, domed ceiling with images of angels and demons painted on its entirety. He tried to move, but found he was unable. Panic started to set in, as he thought this might be a version of a coffin where he was paralyzed and never able to move again.

Then he noticed that his arms were moving of their own accord. He was not controlling them, but they were definitely flailing. One of his hands made its way into his line of sight and Marcus thought it looked babyish. Was he in the body of a baby? How was that even possible, and how exactly was *that* supposed to be helpful? What good would it do him to not be able to move or do anything?

Open your mind. Maria's words invaded his mind, and Marcus thought that he might as well try that, since he couldn't do much of anything else.

An adult appeared over him and stared down at him intently. "How you doing? Are you ready?" A smile perverted by some uncommunicated thought played on the adult's lips. "But you're just a baby. You don't understand a single word coming out of my mouth, do you? I'll be back soon. There are a few more preparations for today's festivities. And when you are older you will thank your mama for this gift." The adult disappeared from view and Marcus went back to staring at the ceiling.

He decided that since he was stuck, he would investigate the ceiling with greater scrutiny. Maybe something in the painting would spark a thought of what he was doing there. No doubt now that he was inside the body of a baby, so he might as well utilize his time wisely.

The painting depicted what looked to be a great war between Heaven and Hell. The angels were bloodied and bruised, holding swords above their heads, and demons with leering smiles on their faces lounged about on the ground. There was the head of a demon under the heels of one of the angels, and a demon held up the remains of an angel's wings.

Whatever was supposed to happen was taking its time, so Marcus tried to figure out exactly where he was and why he was a baby. His first thought was he could be John as a baby, in a room full of people celebrating, what? His birthday? But something about the first adult who hovered over him lent a distinctly ominous overtone to the whole proceeding.

Perhaps it didn't matter what baby he was, he simply needed to witness the scene to gain information. The last theory he entertained, right before his whole preconceived notion of what his life meant came crashing down, was that maybe this baby was related to him in some way, like the man being exorcised.

And then his mother appeared above him, smiling down at him.

His mother, who died giving birth to him, was looking down with excitement in her eyes at this little baby, her baby. It took him a moment to recognize her, because he had only ever seen her in photographs, but once the confusion and initial shock wore off, he believed unequivocally that this was indeed his mother. And he felt something else that was all his own, yet not his own in any way. He sensed the baby's recognition of his mother. It was an intense cognitive response that only infants seem to completely possess. The type of response where even if a mother was one half of an identical pair of twins, their baby would still distinguish between the two with perfect accuracy.

Marcus had always wondered how babies were able to discern differences so easily; what cue they received that informed them that their knowledge was right and good. He had always known that children had sense to know when someone was surrounded by a good aura or had more malevolent intentions, a dark soul. Kids and pets were like divining rods for humanity, but most people chose not to listen, or were too distracted to notice.

He was overwhelmed by the purity of love he felt flowing from this baby and could feel his legs kicking and arms flailing. The love of someone who doesn't understand brokenness and heartache, who doesn't realize that the world takes and destroys what it can in an attempt to eliminate the human spirit. This baby only understood the goodness, the wholeness of life. This was life before the inevitable shattering; before the parent dies or the grown-up corners you with ill-intent or the crushing debt you have racked up gives you life-ending thoughts, or the first love of your life breaks your heart. None of that exists in the universe of an infant well loved, and in some deep part of his psyche, Marcus wished he could remain in this snapshot for all eternity. He didn't want to see what came next; he didn't care what came next. All he wanted to do was look up at his mother and simultaneously envy this baby. And then she spoke, "Hello Marcus.

And, how are you, my darling?"

Marcus's brain split into a million pieces as a whole host of thoughts rushed through his mind like a river whose dam had been shattered.

But she died during childbirth. This can't be real. This is a trick. I don't believe any of this. My father wouldn't have lied to me. The thoughts kept seeping in through the cracks, threatening to tear apart any certainty. It felt like a violation of his personal space. He couldn't control the thoughts, he couldn't mute them, he could only simply let them come and wash over him and hope they would eventually subside so he could become himself again.

The baby, he, Marcus, began to cry. His mother frowned and reached down to stroke his face and tell him everything was all right. Marcus knew that his confusion had caused the discomfort in the baby version of himself. Because they were both him, the psychic connection was strong enough for overflow. If the emotion were intense enough in one, the other could feel it. When he had looked at his mother the emotional crossover occurred, and the influx of thoughts were enough to disturb himself as a baby. This wasn't a dream or some weird drug-induced vision. Any doubt about the reality of what he was experiencing was fading with every second he remained in this place.

Marcus's mother stood up and smiled one more time down at him. "Only a few more minutes and then we will begin. I love you, little man."

I love you too, Marcus thought, apparently strongly enough for the baby to make a sort of cooing sound. A radiant smile returned to his mother's face and she replied, "You love me too? That's wonderful." And then she was out of his field of view. As hard as he tried to will the baby's head to move in search of her, he finally resigned himself that he seemed content to simply lay and look at the ceiling.

A few more minutes passed before anything happened, and then one face after another popped into view. He caught quick glimpses of what they were wearing: Ceremonial garments that flowed into skirts. Now the dream came back to him full force, of people dancing around a baby performing some sort of ritual. The clothing was accurate, the number of adults was exact, and the feelings were the same as in the dream. He imagined that the baby felt something was wrong, but he didn't make a sound. It seemed at times love could place blinders on the instincts of even the smallest human.

Marcus's mother appeared once again, still smiling radiantly. "Here we go, little man. Don't worry, it won't hurt a bit. All you have to do is lie there." She propped him up, as if to see better, then moved off to complete the circle of adults, and slowly they began to dance.

Marcus could hear the swish of cloth as they spun lazily, circles within the circle, all of them moving and flowing together as one. The skirts flowed out and back in rhythm to the collective, almost as if there was a single orchestrator over the whole ritual. They danced above the baby and around him, always keeping the circle closed and always maintaining formation. Marcus had the sense that if they broke even once they would have to start from the beginning. But he was still confused as to what they were doing, and why he was involved. Nothing made any sense.

The first utterance went into the atmosphere, a sort of grunt that pitched up into a scream-like ululation. Then another of them making the sound, and another. The progressive sound made its way around the circle, and the person who had first made the sound made another utterance, similar, but slightly different. This sound started as a growl deep in the throat and rose to the same pitched ululation. Again, it went around the circle. Sound after sound emitted from the deepest places inside the members' souls.

It took Marcus a moment to realize the circle had sped up slightly and continued to do so with each cry's completion through the group. The dance and sounds continued for some time, and just when Marcus felt it would never stop, one of the ranks fell to the ground, convulsing and shaking. It reminded him of those videos he had seen where people had been slain in the spirit at a church. The videos where the Holy Spirit took hold of a person and shook them violently to show them how connected they were with God. His gut told him God wasn't present during this ceremony. His instincts were screaming that there was a much more sinister presence at work.

The group ignored the one that had fallen to the ground and continued to dance. Another person dropped, exhibiting the same symptoms as the first. Marcus was only able to see what was happening out of the corners of his eyes, because the baby wouldn't move his head so he could get a better look. A third member dropped, and now the collective stopped their dance. They gathered around the fallen individuals and began tearing at their clothes. A chant crossed their lips as they did this: *Ad hoc sibi uni tenebris. Subimus obscurum est.* Marcus's knowledge of Latin was somewhat limited, but he found he didn't need to translate, because the same translator came through for him as before: *To the dark one we commit; to the dark one we submit.* They repeated the chant over and over, the volume rising and falling like a wave on the ocean.

Marcus had been curious about what was happening, but as the chanting continued a sense of dread filled his body. A creeping sensation entered his mind, as if something was trying to roost in his head and take up residence there. He tried to shake his head to rid himself of the feeling, but the invisible presence held fast, sliding into every crevice of his awareness. There was nothing he could do but hope to maintain his sanity. It felt like an itch he couldn't scratch.

The baby was feeling it as well because he began to squirm and look around for the first time. That was the first instance Marcus got a clear view of what they were doing with the three that had thrown themselves to the ground. The group had lined them up and seemed to be examining them. No place on the body was sacred. Hands flew over breasts and between folds of skin and into mouths. The three on the ground were one man and two women. And they allowed themselves to be violated in ways that made Marcus's stomach turn. The man was fondled, hands moving up and down, searching; forever searching. The women were examined as intimately as a lover's exploration. Yet through it all Marcus had the distinct notion that none of the ritual was sexual; it seemed to be almost clinical.

After a few minutes, the group stood one by one until they encircled the prone bodies on the floor. The dancing commenced once again, but only for a brief moment. A deep hum invaded the room, and everyone could feel it. A couple people shivered, one let out a moan of pleasure, and another began to weep. Marcus saw his mother move away from the group, and when she returned, she was holding an ornate dagger. She approached the first person on the ground, one of the women, and stood over her. *Offerimus sacrificium purissima pars mortale. We offer up the purest piece of this mortal body as sacrifice.* His mother spoke the words flawlessly, as if she had done it a thousand times. One member of the group bent and pointed to a spot just under the woman's left breast. Marcus's mother bent down with the dagger and as she did the deep hum became an incessant buzz. Marcus watched with horrified fascination as several members' noses began to bleed. They simply stood there, letting the blood flow down their faces.

Marcus's mother pressed the blade against the spot the other had pointed to and she pressed the edge through the skin, pulling the knife as she applied pressure. The knife ran smooth, clearly razor sharp. Rivulets of blood formed in the opening, and then blood was spilling to the ground. One of the others held out a small wooden bowl and caught a fair amount of the blood, but the wound was deep enough that blood continued to flow around the woman onto the ground. But she did not move or flinch. It was almost as if she were in a trance to ensure she was unaware of what was being done to her.

The man lying next to the woman on the ground was next. The words were spoken again: *Offerimus sacrificium purissima pars mortale.* A member of the group pointed high up on the man's thigh, just below his groin, and Marcus's mother made a clear way for her knife. Her incision was identical to the one before. Again, one of them caught some of the blood in the wooden bowl, and then they moved on to the other woman. Marcus's mother sliced into the sole of her foot after repeating the obligatory words, and blood was caught in the bowl once more.

All except the ones on the ground moved toward Marcus. His mother stood in front of him and smiled ruefully. The others began tearing the clothes off her body, and not gently. Marcus felt his defense mechanisms kick in and he tried to strain to protect his mother. But he was trapped.

Suddenly he realized this had all been on purpose. Maria knew what would happen on this visit and she needed to make sure he could witness without interfering. The baby began to cry, afraid for his mother, unable to do anything except watch and Marcus with him.

Once his mother was naked, the other members began their invasive groping. Marcus felt a stirring inside of him when he saw his mother's breasts and imagined an Oedipal side of himself that was connected to the breast-feeding the baby was most likely enjoying at that point in his life. The feeling was quickly replaced when he noticed fingers approaching his mother's sensitive areas. He wanted to close his eyes, but the baby didn't have the awareness yet to feel anger or shame at the act. A groan escaped his throat amidst the cries, but no one noticed. Dread filled that tiny little body, hoping it would be over soon, wishing he could return to the garden room with Maria. He didn't want to be here anymore, no matter the information he was sent to gain.

And then the examination was complete. A man, who Marcus had not realized had been standing behind him, stepped forward and took the blade from his mother. When the man turned Marcus saw it was his father. The father who raised him and loved him and cared for him. The father who never told him about this ritual in which he had participated with his mother. The father who drank himself to death.

One of the members pointed to the right side of Marcus's mother's neck, just below her ear. Marcus's father approached the spot with the tip of the knife, but Marcus felt him hesitate. It seemed his father wasn't fully committed to this ritual, at least not like the others.

The buzz in Marcus's head was growing until it was almost unbearable. Every second his father didn't cut into his mother it got worse. It was an anticipatory insectile purr and, whatever was about to happen was like standing on the edge of a precipice. All that was left to do was leap. The knife tip grazed the porcelain skin of his mother, but it was unsteady. Marcus's father licked his lips and looked at the others. "What if I hit the carotid? She'll bleed out."

One of the oldest of the members stepped forward and put a hand on Marcus's father's shoulder. "Matthias, this is purity. This is divine guidance. You will not cause your wife to die. Please speak the phrase and give us the blood to combine with the others so we may complete the ritual. It is time."

Marcus's father thought about that for a long moment and then slowly nodded. He took a deep, shuddering breath, uttered the phrase *Offerimus sacrificium purissima pars mortale* and sliced down along his wife's neck. The blood flowed instantly, and Marcus's father dropped the knife instinctually. One of the others caught the dagger before it hit the ground and walked it over to a firepit Marcus hadn't noticed before. The blade was placed into the fire, the hilt resting outside the flames, so it didn't become unbearably hot. Marcus's mother's blood was caught in the wooden bowl and the person holding the bowl used a wooden stirring stick to mix all the bloods together. *Hostia integra compleretur tuemur. The sacrifice complete, we plead for completion.*

The dagger was retrieved from the fire and one of them went from person to person cauterizing the wounds that had been made. None of them made a sound or flinched as the heat from the side of the blade cooked their skin and staunched the flow of blood. Marcus's mother waited for her turn and when her wound was cauterized Marcus smelled the acrid odor of burning flesh. The group then surrounded Marcus, looking down at him. The eldest of them looked directly into Marcus's eyes, and for a moment Marcus wondered if the man sensed his presence but then dismissed the thought.

"It is time to complete the ritual. Mother and father come forth and finish the incantation over your son. Bless him with this gift. May it serve him well." The old man stepped back to the edge of the circle and Marcus's mother and father stepped forward, holding the bowl of blood.

Marcus had been so transfixed by the ritual that he had forgotten about the feeling that his mind had been infiltrated; a foreign body had made his head its home. And the buzz now sounded like a million angry bees ready to attack the first creature that dared come close. Marcus's head was splitting, yet all he could do was lie there and wait and hope for it to end.

Marcus's mother spoke, "Ad hanc formam nos committere ut in nave rostrate venit. Jacturae lucre gratia accipiatur. Quapropter suscipe benedictionem hanc, et sanctum puerum tuum in animo aperiam in saecula. Sic erit et illud est." *We commit this form unto you as a vessel. We accept the loss in order to gain. Accept this child into your sanctum and open his mind to the unseen. So, it shall be, and so, it is.* She poured the blood onto Marcus's face, and the baby spluttered and cried. Marcus could taste the coppery flavor of the blood as it ran down his throat. He tried to gag but found himself unable.

No one helped the baby; they started up their dance again. His mother and three others naked, the rest in their costumes. Abruptly, the baby stopped crying and Marcus felt the new inhabitant in his head speak to him: *I will show you the universe and it will not destroy you. This is my gift to you. Open up to me and you will see anything you desire.*

Who are you? Marcus tried to ask the question, but either the thing in his head didn't hear or chose not to respond. The penny-copper taste in his mouth was subsiding, and everything appeared to be returning to normal, aside from the pressure in his head and the people dancing their frenzy. The buzzing subsided and Marcus was wondering when he would be returning to the garden room when the vibration began.

It was hardly noticeable at first, but quickly grew into something horrific. Marcus felt as though his teeth were going to rattle out of his head. He could feel it in every fiber of his being, and it was not pleasant. The others were not affected by the reverberation, but Marcus decided he had had enough with new sensations for the day.

He wanted out, and he wanted out now.

The tremor rose in intensity and then stopped. It was gone. There were no residual phantom vibrations, no indication that anything had ever been there in the first place.

Then in the silence, a quiet hissing snaked its way into his mind consciousness. A face appeared in front of his, but Marcus found he could only catch bits and pieces out of the corner of his eye. The voice entered his head and whispered venomously to him. *You are mine. You belong to me. I will show you the universe, but it will destroy you. Make a deal with a demon and there are consequences. You will learn this in time. Now, are you ready?*

Before Marcus had a chance to answer he felt a switch go off in his brain and the room around him darkened. He found himself surrounded by unearthly creatures; hellish creations that made him want to scream. But the wails stuck in his throat and all he could do was stare.

The one that spoke to him had hollow eye sockets and a mouth that gaped showing rows of needlelike teeth. Another, further off, moved along on long clawed hands that left a trail of an oily substance as dark as sin in its wake. It didn't appear to have a head, but that did not hinder it from navigating the space.

The first one appeared again at the forefront of his mind and Marcus knew the creature could clearly see him. Something vaguely resembling a smile passed across its face.

"It is nice to meet you face-to-face Marcus. We are one and the same now. We are one being. Your body; your soul has nurtured me for many years. I am grateful for that. You are a host among hosts."

Marcus tried to look away, the sense of utter violation churning his stomach. But, as the entity had said, they were entwined. Connected at a level that would likely kill the host if ever separated.

Then he looked at his mother and saw a creature wrapped around her body, in her body, through her body, and it fed from the cauterized wound in her neck. Marcus could hear a sickly slurping sound coming from the beast and when it raised its head, he saw that the mouth ended in a proboscis not unlike a hypodermic needle. The unholy monstrosity looked directly at Marcus and hissed. Then it turned back to his mother and resumed its meal. The voice spoke once more in his head:

"My brethren have existed for eternity, and your bloodline is pure enough to withstand our presence. Your mother's soul resides beside me in the darkest part of Hell. Wail for her soul. Scream for her damnation."

And Marcus began to scream.

CHAPTER 9

The scream followed Marcus back to the garden room, and he leapt up from his chair, knocking it over. He moved toward a corner of the room, his hands pawing at his face, sure they would come away slick with blood.

"What in the…what…I…that can't be real. It's not real. What did they do to me? WHAT DID THEY DO TO ME?!!"

Maria remained calm, stirring her tea, and watched him panic for another few seconds before saying anything.

"They imbued you with the ability to see the otherworld." She stated it in a matter-of-fact tone that instantly made Marcus irate.

He moved toward her, pointing his accusatory finger again.

"Is that what they did? Using what, demon possession? Who does that to their own child? Their baby?!" His voice was rising, but he didn't seem to notice. "That's child abuse! That's…worse than child abuse!"

Maria patiently waited for him exhale his fury. Marcus huffed and puffed around the room, looking for something, anything, he could throw, or better, break. He chose the fine china teacup still sitting near the chair he had overturned. Purposefully, he walked to the table, grabbed the teacup, and as he drew his arm back to throw, he made eye contact with Maria. His resolve weakened, and he clutched and unclutched the teacup compulsively a few times before setting it carefully back on the table. Still Maria waited for him to sort it out in his head.

"You knew about this. You knew this waited for me, and you didn't warn me. How dare you!" His voice broke, his resolve faltering. "How dare you."

Maria offered a sympathetic smile. Again, Marcus felt rising rage, but this time he fought it. He needed answers. As he took some deep breaths to calm himself, Maria spoke.

"I told you there were things you would have to see for yourself. If I sat here and told you what you would witness, you would maybe believe a tenth of what I said. Maybe. Probably not. Words cannot adequately express what only experience is able." She took a deep breath, sipped at her tea, and finished with, "So calm down and I'll explain some things, now that you have a baseline."

With a sigh, Marcus righted his chair and sat down. His mind was a tumbling, rushing river of questions and jumbled information. He was unable to hold onto even one question long enough to articulate the thought. It was there, and then it catapulted out of his head like an unmanned raft navigating rapids. So, he closed his eyes and focused again on his breathing. In through the nose; out through the mouth. Rhythmic. Slowing. Soothing.

"Are you done?" Maria finally asked.

"Don't treat me like a child," Marcus spat back venomously.

"Not my intention. I just need you to be focused so I can fill in some gaps. Maybe give you a little closure on some matters."

Internally, Marcus scoffed, but kept his comments to himself. He breathed deep a few more times and then nodded at Maria, giving her permission to explain.

"What your parents, and the others, put you through is called the Ritual of Amdusias. He is a Duke of Hell that has a horn on his head like a unicorn. Although the horn has been described more like a proboscis. His ability to bring forth familiars is what they used to marry your mind to the otherworld. The voice you heard in your head was the sealing of the ritual, and what left you with your gift of discernment.

"Your parents believed that darkness could be fought with darkness. *Know thy enemy to destroy thy enemy.* They had great plans for you, and I would say you have used your talents wisely. However, your father never quite came to terms with what they did that day. The drinking was a result of his conflicted soul. He had no other way of dealing with it.

"Your mother stayed for a few more years; long enough to bear a third child; your younger brother. But the ritual left its mark on her as well."

"Amdusias." Marcus said the name, allowing it to roll over his tongue. The name felt like poison.

"I saw him. He stuck his horn into my mother's neck, feeding on her." Marcus sounded defeated.

Maria nodded sadly. "Have you heard of the term *duality*?"

She waited until Marcus whispered, "I've heard it."

"In this case, your mother's duality, her fracture occurred deep in her soul. She lost part of herself to the demon when she endorsed you as a seer. Because of that she wasn't content with simply living out life waiting to see what you would become. She took your brother when he was an infant and left. And to answer your unspoken question, she died a few years ago."

"And my brother?" Marcus asked quietly.

"He's out there, doing his own thing. I know you probably want to find him, but he is a fragile person, prone to mental breakdowns. I don't think you suddenly reappearing in his life is going to do him any favors."

A thought occurred to Marcus. "My sister didn't die from a horse kick, did she?"

For the first time, Maria hesitated. She looked deep into Marcus's eyes, hoping he sensed that she felt it was better for him to leave this one alone. He didn't budge. "No."

"What happened?" Again, Marcus felt his world unraveling. Everything he thought he had known was a lie. His childhood was a sham, and it was all because of his parents.

Maria hesitated again and Marcus slammed his open palm against the table, rattling her teacup. "Tell me."

"Your parents wanted to make sure you were strong."

"What happened to my sister?" Marcus asked again, with more insistency.

"That's why they performed the ritual, as awful as that is."

"I'm not sightseeing. Give me an answer." He began to shake.

"As an infant your sister was possessed by a demon. Your lineage precludes you to be unusually sensitive to the otherworld. Your mother studied the occult, and based on ancestry on your father's side, she made discoveries and opened doors. Most likely she didn't mean to, but she invited a demon into your sister. Maybe she knew what she was doing, or maybe she was trying to prove that it was all a load of hocus pocus nonsense. That I don't know. But..." Maria took a long, shuddering breath, "Your sister was not strong enough to withstand the exorcism. Your mother unwittingly summoned an extremely powerful demon. Maria died in her crib with your mother and father and a Priest standing over her, torn apart when the Priest commanded the demon to remove itself from her."

Marcus felt himself sinking, his muddled thoughts incoherent, and emotions fluctuating moment to moment. Despair settled deep in his chest, and he could taste bile rising in his throat.

Was Maria playing some sort of game? She had to be. This was all a horribly, sick perverted joke. There was no way he couldn't have known about this ritualistic history and abuse if it had really occurred. He was being played.

This was how he tried to reconcile his experience, but his heart was unconvinced. They were justifications covering reality. After all, it framed and explained everything he had experienced throughout his life.

"Because of your line of descent you were more susceptible to influence, and your parents took advantage of that. And," she paused, "I'm sorry they did it."

She waited another moment before continuing. "Selfishly, I'm glad they did. Because now, maybe, you can help my children with the *Dark Man*."

When Marcus looked up, he could see tears standing in her eyes, but wouldn't release down her face. He gently reached for a cloth napkin and handed it to her.

"Who is the *Dark Man?*" Marcus asked the question anticipating no real response. He got exactly what he expected.

"After this third, and last, journey I am sending you on you are going to need my help. The *Dark Man* is growing stronger, and I don't know how much longer I will be able to fend him off on my own. You saw the mark on Charlie's ankle. Evil has an uncanny ability to gain power, but it can be fooled. That phrase *Pride cometh before a fall* relates very well to evil. True faith is trust; it's a matter of trusting in something that actually matters, something that's pure instead of something sinister and selfish."

"How is he getting more powerful? Wouldn't you become more powerful as well? Is the *Dark Man* a demon?" Marcus felt his gray matter reactivating and thoughts swirled. Nothing made sense; everything seemed wrong.

"That's the thing about the otherworld. It is a dark, twisted realm ruled by dark creatures of the netherworld. You know the other phrase *the wages of sin is Death?* This is spiritual death. The palpable delusion of separation from God. Such a choice is profound and rightfully within the authority of being human; this choice of self-willed, independence and crafting of aloneness. As coerced and infected as free will might be, it continues to exist even after physical death. That free will has the power to create the illusion of separation." Maria never broke eye contact with Marcus as she spoke. There was a deep sadness in her eyes.

Marcus was slowly beginning to understand the implications, and he filled in the rest. "And the demons dwell in the landscape of the otherworld, making bargains with those who choose to defile their souls even more, for more power, more independence. These deals and alliances give the sinister spirits a demonic strength. What a trap we have perpetrated on ourselves."

He thought of his parents. "What do they also say? '*The road to hell is paved with good intentions?*'"

Maria nodded.

Marcus was still processing, but his mind was back in its own place, and that at least made him feel better. What Maria was telling him made sense, but that feeling of dread still held sway in the pit of his stomach. It was likely that she was still holding back pertinent information until she considered it the right time. Hadn't she said as much?

He was in too deep but he knew that if he didn't follow through regardless of how it might end, he would be haunted by not knowing the rest of his life. As much as he wanted to click his heels three times and zip on back home, he knew he was stuck, and yes, by damned choice.

"Until death do us part," Marcus muttered under his breath.

"What do you mean?" Maria asked sincerely.

"This whole situation is like some sort of psychotic marriage arrangement. Our lives, yours and mine, are now interwoven in such a way that if I leave now it will have the same feeling as cheating on you and taking all the assets for myself."

Marcus furrowed his brow, trying to make sense of what he was saying.

"None of this is fair. It's not fair to you, and it's not fair to me. It certainly isn't fair to your children. My dad always used to say that life wasn't fair, but justice and righteousness would somehow prevail. I think I understand what he meant now. But I'm not certain he was right."

Maria looked grieved by his words. "I am truly sorry that I dragged you into this shit-storm. But, I am selfish and desperate and I believe you are the only one that has the power to do what needs to be done."

She broke the ensuing silence with a grimace. "Help me Obi-Wan Kenobi?"

Marcus smiled and sighed. "I'm your only hope."

He looked at the table in front of him. On it sat the box. He would never use a trinket box like this one, ever again in his life; they were forever like the street he avoided.

He smiled a little at the thought. *Life's not fair, but justice and righteousness will prevail? Thank you very much and a nice day to you too.*

He opened the box and pulled out a candle, already lit. Marcus glanced up at Maria as he slid away.

CHAPTER 10

The room in which Marcus landed was intensely dark. He could hear the soft murmur of a voice in another room but couldn't make out any words. He stood still, waiting for his eyes to adjust. It only took a few moments, but he realized he was unexpectedly standing in the kitchen of the house where his physical body was currently sitting, silently, hopefully with his eyes closed.

He peeked out into the garage, assuming this wasn't a concurrent time frame, but needing this verified. Not surprisingly, his body wasn't there, and the garage was empty.

The voice continued mumbling from another room, so Marcus decided to find it. It was on entering into the living room that he noticed the entire house was dark. There were no lights on, but it was more than that. The house itself felt dark; even sinister. Uneasiness settled in Marcus's stomach as he made his way down the hall toward the master bedroom and its open door. As he approached the voice grew louder, until he could almost make out what was being said. An undulating flicker appeared, and when he turned and stepped across the threshold, he saw nearly fifty candles placed throughout the room, giving off the only light in the entire house. His first thought was, *I really hope it's not Valentines.*

But it was only John, sitting at a desk talking on a cell phone. Finally, Marcus was able to catch his side of the conversation.

"I understand. No. Please, take as much time as you need with your sister. I'm looking forward to seeing you and the kids, but I know you aren't feeling well." A pause as John listened to the voice on the other end. "I love you too, Maria. And I'm fine. I've got frozen pizza and beer. Bachelor's paradise."

He smiled, and Marcus caught a glimpse of the man he had been before his wife had died. Possibly, he and John might have even been friends in another life. Tragedy splits open the fabric of humanity in different ways, and sometimes it leaves its victims in the dirt without a hand to help them out. Marcus felt this is what had happened to John.

"I will see you in a few days. Rest up, and please don't drive if you feel faint. I need you to be safe."

Pause.

"Okay. Love you too. Yep. Bye."

John pressed *End* on his phone and sitting back, took a deep breath.

Moving toward him, Marcus saw that he had a laptop open and, before John closed the lid, Marcus recognized the image of a pentagram. That was unexpected and odd.

Suddenly, for Marcus the room came completely into view. Darkness and an array of candles laid out with precision and plan, and a place in the center of the lights where John had torn up the carpet revealing hardwood floors beneath. There was drawn a Pentagram, with candles at all its points. A kitchen knife lay in the middle of the circle.

Under his breath, Marcus whispered, "Shit!" He was about to witness *another* ritual. It seemed one wasn't enough.

A second realization hit Marcus: John was going to try and summon the *Dark Man*. But why? Why would he put his children in danger? It made no sense. There was no reason for this man to summon some malevolent spirit into his house, unless—

Meanwhile, John had taken off his shirt and kneeled on the ground in the center of the circle. He moved the knife to his side and pulled a paper out of his back pocket. Leaning over his shoulder, Marcus could make out instructions on how to perform a summoning.

John placed the paper on the floor in front of him and smoothed it out. He started mumbling to himself, reading the directions. "I probably should have memorized this," John said to no one, and then laughed. His laugh made Marcus jump and then all the hairs on his body stood on end.

Something was tickling the back of Marcus's mind. Something that would make sense of all this. But try as he might, he couldn't put his finger on what it was.

It lingered just outside of his grasp, the sort of thought that would find an answer as he dozed off to sleep. But this was urgent, and he played with like a wet knot.

What was it John had said earlier? They had been talking about the house and walking through while the children were watching their show. If he was performing a summoning, then he was trying to contact someone who was dead. But he had been talking to his wife on the phone. Obviously, she was still alive. If not her, who?

John reached for the knife and held out his left hand. He was nearing the end of the ritual, and it caught Marcus off guard. But even as a sense of panic kept rising, Marcus knew there was nothing he could do but watch.

Who was it John had mentioned that had died? Marcus shifted from one foot to the other as if he had to pee, as if such movement might loosen his thoughts and give him the answer.

At that moment, John picked up the piece of paper and read aloud, "Craig, I ask of thee to come forth and commune with me. I ask of thee to enter my home so that we may speak."

Craig? While the name seemed familiar to Marcus, it was fairly generic, like John. He couldn't recall anyone he knew with that name.

John drew the knife across his hand, slicing open his palm, making a deep cut that poured blood immediately. He then moved from candle to candle on each point of the pentagram and doused the flames with his dripping blood. He looked woozy as he reached the final candle, and it took him multiple attempts to douse the last flame.

John then sat in the middle of the drawing and pulled a rag out of his pocket with his non-bloodied hand. He wrapped the rag around the crude incision and waited. Nothing happened. He picked up the paper with the instructions, re-read it, and placed it back on the floor.

Marcus closed his eyes and walked back through his prior conversations with John, trying to force himself to remember who it was that John had said.

In a sudden rush Marcus remembered it all. He knew who John was attempting to call forth, and if he was correct, this person was the *Dark Man*. He looked at John, slumped on the ground, losing hope that his ritual would work, and, even knowing John couldn't hear him, Marcus shouted, "It's your brother!"

In an instant, any remaining warmth dissipated from the room, extinguishing the remaining candles as it left. The bathroom mirror shattered as a sense of power and presence arrived with a bone-shivering chill.

Marcus was certain John had no idea what he had just welcomed into the physical realm of his home. Like a blanket, a sense of hopelessness dropped on Marcus, but John was giddy. He had succeeded and was thrilled!

It made sad sense that if John wanted to speak to his brother and his ritual worked he would be ecstatic, but surely, he must feel the evil now entering the room.

As the invisible entity slowly arrived, Marcus found it increasingly difficult to breathe. He took a step back but remained just inside the room. If this all went belly up his flight response was ready.

Marcus even held his breath. It felt like the room was being searched by something looking for a home.

"Dammit," exclaimed John, snapping Marcus out of his trance.

Standing up, John walked quickly to a nearby dresser and grabbed a baby monitor. He then sat down in the center of the pentagram, flipped on the monitor, and took a deep breath.

The only sound that filled the room was the white noise sound of static droning through the monitor. Marcus felt an increasingly strong urge to run. He fought it, knowing he needed to understand everything that was happening here.

"Craig?" John asked tentatively. Static. Nothing. He tapped the monitor a couple times as if that might help.

"Craig?" John asked again softly. Again, nothing. Marcus shifted uncomfortably, wanting to be anywhere but here.

And then a slight change in the pattern of the static. Quickly John held the monitor to his ear, listening intently.

And from it came a soft, breathy hissing voice.

"Joohnnn."

The name was drawn out, as if a snake was on the other end. At this point, Marcus wasn't convinced that it wasn't a snake that John was communicating with.

"I'm here," John said, enthusiastically. "I'm here, Craig!"

"Joohnnn. Why am I here?"

Even though the monitor's static clipped the words there was enough to gather what Craig was saying.

"Uh, Craig, I need closure. I need to ask you a few questions and then I will let you rest. So, *I* can rest."

"What questions?"

Craig sounded genuinely perturbed that John would have the audacity to summon him. The sense of dread strengthened, and Marcus took another instinctive step backwards, one foot outside the room.

John cleared his throat. "Did you really do those things? I mean, did you...what they said, was it true?"

Marcus cocked his head to one side. John hadn't mentioned anything about his brother being involved in any nefarious activities. Perhaps he hadn't thought it relevant. He made a mental note to ask John when he returned to his physical body.

"I need you to do something for me."

Craig ignored the question. It seemed he had his own agenda.

This is when Marcus realized that the invitation John had offered to his brother may even have been orchestrated by his brother in some way. He wasn't aware of a way for a dead person to truly communicate without consent, but maybe there was a way to leave subtle hints to guide a person in a desired direction. It certainly appeared that Craig was prepared for this encounter.

"You didn't answer my question. Did you do those...things?" But even though John stuck to his question, Marcus could tell his resolve was failing.

The house shuddered, as if the cold had reached its old bones and was shivering.

John made a weak squeaking noise and lost his nerve. A puddle of urine pooled underneath him, and his mouth worked up and down, but no sound came out.

"The man responsible for this; track him down, bring him here, and kill him."

John looked out into the room with confusion on his face. "You expect me to kill someone? I am not going to kill anyone."

Craig shook the house again, and John looked as if he were trying to fold in on himself.

"You will do it!"

John tried to compose himself, but the pee staining his pants and running onto the carpet had taken from him any luxury of dignity.

Marcus was trying to figure out exactly where the dark energy in the room was located. He figured there had to be a central spot from where the spirit was operating. But, even as he tried to pinpoint the source point, he felt it ebb and flow from one area in the room to another. One second it was behind John, the next it was over the bed, and then it was right next to him, to his left.

Marcus looked that direction and concentrated, trying to see any trick of the light or shimmer that might indicate the spirit. But there was nothing. The best he was able to do was catch a glimpse of something out of the corner of his eye, but when he turned and looked, there was nothing. But Marcus felt Craig linger near where he was standing for a long moment before moving elsewhere in the room.

"Pull yourself together, little brother."

John was breathing deeply, panicking. He was concentrating on something; maybe trying to close the door he had opened.

But then Marcus had another thought, one that discouraged him greatly, and it was instantly confirmed. Craig's presence was still in the house. *John doesn't know how to close the door.*

The room tilted and Marcus felt he might vomit and pass out like a junkie on an overdose. He was certain he was right. He also knew the longer the presence remained in the house the stronger it would become. Maria had told him as much.

Marcus composed himself, far better than John was managing to at the moment and stepped through the situation. Only a few days prior he had received a call from John and told there was a presence in his home. Once he was at the house, he sensed the presence of two spirits from the Otherworld. He had been speaking with Maria, who told him that she sent for him to help. And now there was someone else that John was supposed to bring to the house. Did John succeed? Was there a body buried somewhere that he would find if he kept digging? Was Craig murdered?

None of it made any sense. The whole story unraveled itself and wove itself anew in Marcus's mind. Articles of declaration shifting and twisting to create a new narrative. And he had a feeling that this wasn't the end of the blind corners. He had a sense that by the end of this day the story would be entirely different; that itch that kept scratching somewhere near the back of his consciousness.

His thoughts whirled so strongly that it took him a moment to realize that John was looking intently around the room. Instinctively he held his breath and caught the last two words coming from the baby monitor:

"*—is here?*"

"Just the two of us. No one else is here." John continued to scan the room, looking for any indication that he was wrong on this point, but he clearly didn't see or sense Marcus's presence.

For Marcus, alarm bells went off all the same because Craig *had* sensed his presence. It was probably only a matter of time until he was discovered. He had no clue what would happen if he was caught outside of his own time in the Otherworld by a spirit. He was fairly certain that any of the demons he encountered in the other visions would have done something to him if they could, but he had no desire to find out it didn't apply here. So, he took another step back and inadvertently let out a soft groan.

Everything stopped. His groan was audible on the monitor. It was soft, but John had heard it and was now looking at it intently. Marcus felt a rush of putrid, hot air approach him and he almost saw a face in the air, but it vanished as quickly as it appeared. He tried to edge around the doorframe, but found himself frozen and unsure of what would happen next. That was when he heard the murmur next to his left ear, and the voice projecting through the baby monitor simultaneously:

"You little idiot! You let someone else through! Someone else is here, you little shit! I knew I couldn't trust you with this! Your head is full of loose marbles, banging against each other!"

Sitting on the floor, John's mouth moved up and down, unable to defend himself. That was probably for the best as Marcus had the feeling that if John said anything, Craig would have hurt him.

Marcus did experience a small piece of relief. Craig didn't know who the other presence was, in spite of the bit of audio that transmitted through the monitor. If Craig had known who, it was likely that both he and John would be in extreme danger.

That's when Marcus felt an even deeper cold creep over his skin. Craig was reaching out, trying to pull him into the same plane of existence; pull him fully into the Otherworld. The fingers felt like hundreds of maggots trying to burrow their way into his skin, a cold so intense it turned from icy to burning in an instant.

Now Marcus began to panic. He could feel Craig reaching out for his mind, his soul. An unending sense of dread filled his body, and he knew he was going to die here. Die wasn't quite the correct term. He would end here. His being would cease to exist. And that frightened Marcus more than anything. *The wages of sin is death.* He was trespassing where he didn't belong. And he wasn't sure he could return to his rightful place before Craig decimated him.

A moment of pure clarity hit Marcus, and another piece of the narrative clicked into place: *She wants me to invite him in in order to defeat him.* He shook his head and felt lucidity slipping away. He could physically see his sanity like an eel in dark water, slithering away from his grasp. He reached out for it, but the strength of the *Dark Man* held fast. Marcus did the only thing he could think to do as the last shred of himself remained. He screamed.

"Get me out of here! Now! Or I end!" The static rose to a whine on the monitor and John covering his ears, John dropped the monitor, breaking it in the same instant.

For a moment everything felt as if it were suspended in a vacuum. Time stopped, gravity stopped, it all stopped. His eyes closed, and Marcus had the vague sensation that his body was convulsing, but he was disappearing, dismantling. His soul was no longer his. And he heard the voice one last time slither out through the broken baby monitor before it died for good:

"I found you, you son of a bitch!"

The world slipped and tumbled around Marcus; he felt objects around him but couldn't see them. He heard someone screaming and it took him a moment to realize he was hearing his own terror. Inky blackness filled an endless void, and Marcus plunged into it; he felt it rise to meet him as he plummeted, as if the inky black was the well of non-being in which he was drowning.

Then suddenly, instead of being consumed, rage filled the atmosphere. Marcus had presumed he had at least somehow escaped Craig's grasp, but the creature wasn't willing to give him up that easily.

Marcus was overwhelmed by a sudden hatred and fury. He wanted to kick Maria in the teeth the next time he saw her...if he saw her. He wanted to shake John until his neck snapped for being such a fool; bringing his brother back into the physical realm. Everything was wrong; nothing was right. He didn't want to disintegrate on account of this stupid little family, a family that he had only met today. How dare they put their problems on him? How impudent to assume he was willing to risk himself for *them*. The rage flowed in and through him; he seethed with pure, unadulterated hatred.

The feeling of slipping sideways began again. He disappeared into it thinking that this was it, the moment they'd all been waiting for, the end of the existence of Marcus Grimm.

CHAPTER 11

Marcus sat at the table, eyes closed, mouth trembling for a long time. His breath hissed between his teeth, and a tear traced its way down his face and fell to the table. Maria chewed on her lower lip, anxiously.

Finally, after what felt like an eternity, Marcus's eyes flew open and Maria could see the anger and hatred that filled them. In the next instant Marcus was on his feet, the chair beneath him flung with such force that he shattered two panes of glass near the door to the backyard past the Garden Room.

"What the hell was that? He almost caught me? He almost grabbed me!"

Maria sat still, allowing the indignation to burn through him. She knew it would end soon enough, but he had to get it all out, like venom from a snake. If he left even a little behind, he would still be poisoned, but if he vomited every last drop it would be gone and out; let the bad air out.

"He had me. I felt his filthy, rotted fingers all over me. He invaded my mind. If you think I want anything to do with your family now you are gravely mistaken, you pretentious bitch!"

The words didn't even seem to be aimed at Maria anymore. Marcus was spewing words to release it, to rid himself of it. It all smelled and felt like death to him. He sensed that this rage came from another place, from another person, from the owner of the maggoty, groping fingers.

"He's still in my mind. He's screwing with my head. He's trying to drive me insane."

Marcus paced the floor, not caring that he was knocking over pots and plants as he went. His breath was ragged, and his eyes were rimmed with red. He looked on the verge of breaking down and weeping. To be honest, he did feel like crying but knew it was simply a byproduct of the mad energy. Throughout his life, whenever he was intensely angry, he would cry. He didn't know the reason for it, just that it happened. The heightened emotions untethered multiple pieces of him. His pacing stopped, he turned to look at Maria, and yelled.

"AAARRGGHHH!" before collapsing to the floor into a cloud of dust. And that quickly is gone.

His breathing slowly returned to normal, and he found it difficult to raise his head from his chest. From somewhere above him, Maria spoke.

"Are you done now?" Her voice was soft and tender.

Marcus nodded once and sat up. He sniffled, his eyes burning in their sockets.

"Sorry I called you a bitch," Marcus offered weakly.

"You were under the influence of my brother-in-law. You were touched by the rage that is boiling within him. But you are a smart one, Mr. Grimm. You let it all out. None of it remains, which means you can now think clearly." Maria sat in her chair and gestured for Marcus to join her.

Marcus stood up, dusted himself off, and sat in the only other chair that remained at the table. Immediately, questions and thoughts flooded his mind.

"I am not inviting that into my head. You can put that to bed right now."

She held up her hands in a defensive position. "We will get to that. But I believe you have some questions for me."

Marcus shook his head and scowled. "Not if it all leads to *that* end game. If *that's* the final act, you can count me out. He would destroy me."

Maria looked at Marcus patiently and tapped the table with her hand. "How about you ask me your questions and we go from there." It was more a statement than a question.

Marcus stared at her for a full minute before speaking. "Did your husband kill someone?"

"Not yet."

"So, he hasn't gone through with it?"

"He didn't know who he was supposed to bring to the house."

"So, I can still save his or her life. If I can prevent John from bringing this person to the house, I can stop it."

Maria shrugged, and with a small wave of her hand stated, "He knows who it is now."

"How? Did Craig help him figure it out?" Marcus felt that itching at his brain again but pushed it aside. He had important information to gather.

Maria shook her head. "I helped him."

Marcus looked at her confused, but she said nothing else. He felt anger rising back into his chest, but instead of letting it free, sat back and focused. It only took him another minute to put the pieces in order.

"Crap! You got *me* to come to the house. You helped John find *me*, and you helped him get *me* here." His voice was almost a whisper.

Maria smiled sadly and nodded her head. "And now he knows you were there in the room with him and John. A risk I had to take to show you everything."

It still didn't make any sense to Marcus though. He scratched his head and furrowed his brow.

"What did I do to John's brother? How am I responsible for this? I don't understand."

"You will. But first I need you to agree to the steps that must be taken to finish this whole shitstorm. I want my children to be safe, and as long as Craig remains there is no hope for that." Maria suddenly looked very tired, certainly exhausted from the war she had been waging.

"Well," Marcus began resolutely, "I'm not going to fight your battle for you. I have no vested interest in your family. And what it seems like you are about to ask me is nothing short of sacrifice myself for you. Why would I do that? I just met you. And besides, you're dead." Marcus spat the words at Maria with not a little malice and was satisfied to see they actually affected her.

She maintained her composure and replied softly, "You are right. You owe my family nothing. And what I am asking you to do is clearly beyond the realm of sanity; there's no other way of putting it truthfully. But you are the only one I have found that could possibly pull this off. I've already run out of options, and now time. Craig has physically hurt my son! He isn't going to stop. I'm not strong enough alone to withstand this malevolence. If you refuse to help me, I don't know what I'll do. I see no other options."

Her voice cracked and she looked on the verge of breaking down, but with a deep breath gathered herself.

Can ghosts even cry? Marcus thought to himself. *At this point, probably!* After all the events of the day he wasn't certain of much anymore.

Despite all the internal warnings shaking his body, he took his own deep breath and responded, "I will hear you out, but I promise nothing. If this is as dipped in lead as it feels, I'm out. I'm done."

Maria nodded her head. "Fair enough. But you have to agree to hear me out; every word, every syllable."

For a moment Marcus simply stared at her, then sighed and nodded. Maria released the breath she had been holding.

"Okay. What happens next is not good. And you're right, it is definitely dipped in lead as you so eloquently pointed out." She took a beat before adding, "Especially for you. But I have an argument for why it is mutually beneficial, and I genuinely believe you will agree in the end."

Maria fidgeted, putting her thoughts in order. She took another deep breath and began.

"When I discovered I had cancer I started to put away some money every month. I wouldn't say it was a lot, but it was significant enough that it would make an impact. I figured it would be for my kids, but things don't always work out the way you hope.

"The cancer got worse, and I felt myself getting weaker every day. I still socked away the money. I made sure of that. It became evident that I was worsening quicker than the doctors said I would, but I also know that such estimates are often informed guesses at best. But it felt like something wasn't right. The cancer was spreading through my organs, attacking them aggressively. I had lung cancer and never smoked a day in my life. Isn't that a hell of a thing?"

Maria stared off into space, recollecting the last bit of her life, a deep well of emotion spilling from her eyes. Ghosts could cry.

"You know, I didn't even think he was capable of it. I get it. You watch someone you love suffer, and you want to end that for them. It makes sense. I heard him on the phone with the doctors pleading, asking if there was anything that could be done; anything at all. Those phone calls never ended with hope. My breathing was more labored, I lost all my hair, I stopped my treatments and I could hardly walk to the door without needing to rest."

She hesitated before pressing on.

"One day, I told him I was going to take a nap, not unusual, but my mind wouldn't stop moving. I closed my eyes, I willed myself to sleep, but it wasn't happening. I got out of bed and made my way to the kitchen. I thought maybe a nice cup of chamomile would help and as I rounded the corner, I saw John was already making a cup of tea. He had a dropper in his hand, squeezed a few drops into the tea and then stirred it. I thought maybe it was sweetener, until he instinctively lifted the spoon to his mouth but stopped himself, shook his head, and tossed the spoon into the sink with enough clatter for me to escape back to my room undetected. A minute later he knocked on the door softly to let me know he had made me some tea."

"He was poisoning you." Marcus couldn't help himself. He felt his usual ability to maintain emotional distance evaporating.

"Yeah. And you said you would let me say my peace, so shut up." She said it with good humor, and Marcus settled and remained silent.

"He sat and watched to make sure I drank the whole cup. I don't know when he started to poison me but only a week later, I was dead. Please understand, I have no malice toward my husband. He did what he thought would help. Maybe his wonderful brother convinced him it was the right thing to do."

She saw the question in Marcus's raised eyebrows and answered, "Yes. I knew he was in the house by that point. My husband may be a bit headstrong and dim, but he is a pussycat. He told me about how he summoned his brother, and how his presence was still in the house. But I was already too weak to fight back or do anything about it.

"I died and decided that I had to stay to protect my children. So, I didn't cross over. I don't regret it, not for even a moment. But there is only so much I can do in the position I'm in. I am not strong enough to keep fighting him. And if he wins, I lose everything. I assumed that you were the one Craig was referring to, because I read the articles and watched the news coverage. I knew what had happened, and you made the right call with everything."

Marcus looked at her, confused, thinking she had mistaken him for someone else, but didn't say a word. He wasn't ready to be admonished again for speaking out of turn.

"I understand that this is a selfish act, but sometimes we have to act selfishly to protect our own. And I debated whether or not to get you here and try and explain all this to you until I saw the mark on Charlie's ankle. That sealed it for me. That…unholy fiend touched my kid and that is unacceptable."

Maria sighed, readying herself to list out the rest of the steps. Marcus sat still and silent, waiting for the shoe to drop.

"I need you to take me with you through the rest of this. You must allow me to be inside of you or we will not be strong enough to stop Craig. When we go back, you will talk to Charlie, find out anything he might know about the *Dark Man*. I don't think he knows it's his uncle, but I want to make sure. After, you will excuse yourself to get any last readings throughout the house and yard. You need to be alone. I don't care how you accomplish this; give John some line about needing the purity of the energy to speak to you or something. I have a couple places I need you to see that will fill in the last details and explain why you are here."

Maria hesitated and Marcus understood that this last part was the hard part; the part that would make or break the deal. Marcus felt a cold chill travel up his body and into his head.

"In order to stuff my brother-in-law back into his bottle, in order to stop him from whatever he is planning, we will reach out to him and invite *him* into your mind just like you invited me into your mind."

Maria paused to gauge Marcus's reaction, but he revealed nothing.

She continued, "You will keep Craig and me inside your mind. He will be unable to escape, but we have to work together to keep him locked away."

Still no expression on Marcus's face. Maria wasn't certain he was understanding what she was saying.

"Have you ever seen or met someone with dissociative identity disorder? They used to call it schizophrenia or multiple personalities. The thing is, sometimes when someone suffers from this it originates with a decision to invite an entity from the Otherworld into their head. Some invite more and more until they lose themselves completely. They bury their own identity under the many personalities inside their mind. One or two intruders will mess with someone's head enough to warrant strange looks from passersby, but when you add more? Terminal insanity."

Despite all that he was feeling, Marcus still kept his poker face, and Maria dropped the other shoe.

"I truly don't know how much doing this will affect you, but considering how strong Craig is, I imagine the effort to contain him could crack your reality...permanently. You will be the person someone visits. Neither of us strong enough. It will take both of us to keep him hidden, and I don't know if we will succeed in secluding him completely, but we have to try. We need to imprison him. And the only place that might work is inside of you."

Maria sat back in her chair, breathing heavily. She looked spent, exhausted, almost lost. For his part, Marcus bit his lip to keep from screaming every profanity he knew. In all the information she had dumped on him, the piece that brought him near the brink of hysteria was the idea that he might go insane; as cracked as a cheap mirror in a pawn shop.

He made up his mind. He knew what he was going to do, and he opened his mouth to speak, but Maria held up her hand.

"There is one more piece."

God, he thought, *one more piece.*

"I mentioned that I had been stowing away money when I found out I had cancer. I also said this arrangement could be mutually beneficial. The money is yours if you do this for me. Now, I know you probably won't accept the money, especially if do end up in a padded cell with two people inside your head. But you could send the money to your son; to make sure he has a good life."

Marcus was incredulous. All in one day, to find out he had a brother, and he was a father too?

"I don't have a son. I've never been married. No one ever told me after an encounter that they were pregnant."

"Tracy." Maria spoke the name and watched for Marcus's reaction, which was immediate.

Tracy was a girl he had met when he was guest lecturing at a University, talking about his work in the paranormal. She was a fascinated grad student auditing the course and he was taken by her immediately; the intelligence in her eyes, the way she moved her hips forward slightly when he spoke in class. They had used protection, and she had never reached out to him about any child. Maria could be telling the truth, but she could also be manipulating him to get what she wanted.

"She never told you because she planned on aborting him. She tried to go through with it but turns out your son is a fighter. After the attempt failed, her shame kept her from ever contacting you."

Marcus still sat there, mute and stunned.

"His name is Samuel. You will be able to find him easily enough. I'm sure you could be a part of his life…or not. He won't know if you choose to not reveal yourself."

Maria put her hands on her lap, indicating she was done, opening the floor for his response.

Marcus was so dumbfounded he didn't even know what to say. Finally, he blurted out, "How do I even get this money?"

Maria smiled. "I will tell you that after we have an agreement."

Marcus sat back and for minutes tried to gather his thoughts. He drew on old skills, weighing pros and cons, in this situation mostly cons. Finally, he arrived at the same conclusion he had immediately before Maria had dropped the bombshell.

He leaned forward, smiled sincerely, looked Maria in her eyes and said, "With all due respect, Maria, that was a dirty little hand you just played, and you can go ahead and find yourself that short pier you mentioned earlier. I'm outta here!"

CHAPTER 12

Maria held his gaze, neither anger nor indignation crossing her face. She looked resigned, but not defeated. Even if she had one last trick up her sleeve, an ace in the armpit, his mind was made up. He was done! Enough for one day, or even one lifetime. He wanted to go home, grab a beer, prop up his feet, and watch some mindless television show until he fell asleep. Perhaps he could find a drug to help him forget this day.

"I know what I am asking of you. I do. Before you say no for real, could you take a walk around the backyard for a bit and think it over? Snap decisions oftentimes lead to long term regrets. I don't want your emotions to cloud the vision of what you might do in this situation under different circumstances. Do me this one favor and if you come back to me with the same answer, I will release you from this duty and you can go about your life and never look back. Deal?" Marcus scanned Maria's face for any sign of deception but found none.

He nodded his head, "Fine!" he grumbled, rising from the chair. It only delayed the inevitable. His mind was made up. But he did feel badly for her, enough that he couldn't simply walk away. Instead he headed toward the back door. He wanted to get outside before she could say anything else to solidify her case.

The moment he stepped outside and was met by the cool air he was convinced that his decision was the right one. How could 'getting a breath of fresh air' possibly change his mind? But, he figured he could walk around for a bit, maybe throw some rocks into the stream, act like he was truly conflicted about this whole thing, and then flip her the bird as he walked to his car and out of her life (death). *Thank you very much and a nice day to you too.*

He walked down the small hill toward the embankment of the stream, which babbled, unbothered by his life. The sound eased his mind and he again processed. He may or may not have a son, depending on how much he thought he could trust Maria, especially when she was so desperate. She was in his mind and would know about Tracy, hidden away in some internal locked compartment. She could easily use that information to 'twist his arm.'

He found himself wondering what Tracy was doing with her life and figured he might try and contact her to see how she was. *"And, oh, by the way, how's our son doing?"* He could throw that in for good measure to see the reaction.

Tracy had been the best bed mate of his life, but it was more than that. They had connected in a way he had never with anyone before or since. She understood him and accepted him for how he was, which often meant she would wait out his inward spells. That's what she called them: *inward spells*. He tended to ruminate and disappear for a while. His ears shut off all outside stimuli and he would sit inside his mind and solve problems, or think through a situation, much like he was doing at this very moment.

Tracy would look at him and say, "Uh oh, there goes Marky. Off on another adventure with his inward spell."

He would only vaguely hear her, and sometimes was able to pull himself out to rejoin her in whatever they were doing. The only time she hated it was when it happened while they were making love. That was understandable.

But out here, in nature, he could have a long inward spell, and no one would mind. He could sit out here and ponder the greatest questions of the universe until he was satisfied with the reply and there would be no one to ask where he had gone or why his 'device was deflating' at such an inconvenient time. Tracy wasn't shy; she told it how it was. In a way she reminded Marcus of Maria. The thought made him frown, so he shifted his focus elsewhere.

He remembered the only occasion where, as a boy, his father had attempted to instill in him some wisdom. It was a rare moment of sobriety that he remedied soon after the conversation.

His father had been watching news coverage about some guy who murdered a bunch of folks. The news had stated that he was good-looking and charismatic and that was how he was able to find his victims.

"Deception eats away at the soul," his father had said. "Sure, this guy is good looking, and people like him and want to be around him and help him, but inside he is rotting. There is only so long you can hide your true nature before it spills out of you. If you try and hold it back for too long, it vomits its way out and exposes you to the whole world in one quick beat. Marcus, honesty and integrity will be your best friend throughout your life. As long as you hold on tight to those two things you will never go wrong. Things around you may go belly up but maintain your honesty and integrity and it will all right itself by the end."

Marcus remembered that's when he opened a can of beer before continuing.

"And Marcus, always help people when they need it. Maintaining these two tenets will assist you in deciphering who is true and right and who is dark and deceptive. Know the difference and your path will be straight and narrow."

Marcus now knew that his father had been confessing.

"Hey, we kinda screwed you over when you were a baby, but I don't have the spine to tell you that's what happened, so I'm gonna give you a word to the wise, pat you on the back, and go back to blacking out to try and drown my conscience."

The brook babbled, almost like white noise calming him further. Even so, he was a hapless passenger in the riptide of his own thoughts. And this inward spell was not helping him stay with the logic of abandoning ship. Maria was clever and already knew him well enough to encourage this delay. But there was no way he could allow this other entity, to let Craig invade his head, and live with him there. That was the line, and it was a big, impassable line; like the Wall of China you could see from space.

Marcus frowned, unable to turn the tide of his thoughts. Regardless of the atrocities of his origin, somehow, he had come through relatively unscathed. He wasn't a dark and twisted person by nature and pretending to be heartless would not bury the goodness he knew was a deeper truth inside of him.

He had taken his father's words to heart and had lived by them, and because of that he was here now, again struggling with a resolution on which he had stamped his approval only a few minutes prior. Everything reasonable told him he had to stick with his decision, that his livelihood, if not his life, depended on it. And yet...

Frustrated, Marcus picked up a large stone and turned to heave it into the brook. But just as he was about to throw, he was startled by a family of deer standing a short distance on the other bank, staring at him. The rock slipped from his hand and barely missed his foot. In their midst was the twelve spotted fawn. He opened his mouth to speak, but before he could, a girl behind him whispered loudly, "Look! A family of deer."

Marcus whirled around to a couple and two children having a picnic on his side of the creek. It took Marcus a moment to recognize them. He was staring at Maria and John. They appeared to be a little older and Cynthia and Charlie had definitely grown. He didn't understand. And then he did. "Ah, so here's your Ace, Maria," he muttered under his breath.

Cynthia spoke again, hitting her dad on the arm, "I said look at the deer. Geez, dad. Pay attention."

John smiled and rubbed his arm, pretending like she hurt him. "I see them, Cynthia. They're beautiful. Just like all the deer that wander through our backyard every day and poop in our garden."

Cynthia frowned. "Ewww. Gross."

John shrugged and laughed. "Nature can be gross."

They looked happy. But, obviously, it wasn't real. Maria was dead, so it was some attempt at emotional manipulation that Marcus did not appreciate one bit. This is why Maria wanted him to take a walk, so she could try one last low blow at his human decency to get him to change his mind. He shook his head continued to watch the family. If he *was* being manipulated, he might as well enjoy the show.

John threw a bun at Charlie to get his attention. "Tell your mom what your teacher said today."

Charlie's face flushed with embarrassment. "Daaad. I don't want to. It's not a big deal."

Maria turned to Charlie and stroked his hair. "Tell me, bub. What did your teacher say?"

Charlie sighed and rolled his eyes. "Fine. After fifth period, Mrs. Couch—"

"Charlie, that's rude," John said with a smirk on his face.

"Mrs. Davenport pulled me aside and told me that I was the most gifted student she had seen in forty years of teaching. She told me I could be anything I wanted to be."

John took a bite out of the roll he was holding and spit crumbs as he spoke, "That's not what I mean. Tell your mom the other bit; the important bit."

Charlie rolled his eyes again. "She said she hadn't seen anyone as gifted as me since she taught dad when he was a young whipper-snapper."

John dropped the roll like he was dropping a mic. "Boom goes the dynamite. Smart like his old man. The world can't handle us. We are just that good."

Everyone laughed, and Marcus felt the corner of his mouth lift into a small smile. *This is all so cloyingly sweet,* he thought to himself. *It is so unrealistic. Why did Maria even think I would believe any of this?* And then his question was answered.

Maria turned to Cynthia, who had tears running down her cheek. "Hey now, hey now. What's wrong? You know you're smarter than your dad and brother combined, right?" She was trying to lighten the mood, but it didn't work. The dam broke and Cynthia began to sob. Maria and John looked at each other, concerned. "What's going on, sweet pea?"

It took Cynthia a few minutes to calm herself enough to speak, but finally she looked up at her mom and asked the question that sent chills through Marcus's entire body: "What if it comes back?"

Maria smiled warmly at Cynthia and stroked her hair. "I don't think it will. The doctors said after I went into remission that there was a chance it could return, but the last scan showed no sign of cancer anywhere in my body. It's gone. See ya, wouldn't wanna be ya."

"I was reading on the internet that sometimes cancer comes back even after it seems to be completely gone. What about that?" Cynthia had to ask her questions until she was convinced, and Maria wouldn't stop answering until her daughter was fully satisfied.

"True. But the odds are slim, and you know what I say about worrisome imaginations. Why should we worry about something that doesn't exist? It'll rot ya from the inside out." Maria kissed Cynthia on the head and held her tight against her chest. "Besides, if it ever shows its ugly face around here again, we will beat it into the ground."

Cynthia's breath hitched once as she tried to regain her footing, and she whispered, "Okay. I'll try not to worry about stuff that doesn't exist." They all smiled.

Now that the play was over Marcus felt he had more questions, and turning to head back to the Garden Room, almost ran into Maria. He glanced back and the family was gone from their spot in the grass. Maria took his hand and he let her lead him down a path into the forest.

"It's a hell of a thing what you find out after you die. They were going to do another scan the day I died. That scan would have told us that I was in remission. A year later I would be cancer free. I would have gotten to live my life with my family."

Marcus could find no words.

"That's the thing about knowledge; it can be a terrible privilege and a severe mercy. The term ignorance is bliss gets it so right, but so wrong too. Knowledge can be terrible, but it can also be fulfilling and helpful. To know the truth can either make your heart soar or destroy you from the inside out, depending on how you relate to it, whether you bury and ignore it, or let it speak to you. I gave you true knowledge about how my situation could have played out. It wouldn't have been fair to either of us for me to keep you in the dark. If you do agree to help, you need to know."

They walked on while he processed and marveled at how warm her touch was in his hand, how comforting.

"Sometimes we do things because we believe we know the truth, but really we are simply taking an educated guess. I think a lot of religion works like that. Educated guessing helps us justify life when we don't have science or objective evidence to back up our beliefs. And it's not always a bad thing. I mean, sometimes people get it very wrong, like mass genocide in the name of a god. But, over the long haul, it seems goodness in people tends to prevail, no matter how dark the world becomes. There is no proof that God does or does not exist, and the only way to know for sure is to cross over in that moment after death. I chose not to know in order to stay and protect my children.

She stopped and faced him.

"I'm not asking you to choose to stay behind after you die, I'm asking you to help me now. I don't know what it might mean for your life, now or forever. It is a huge ask, and I will stay true to my word if you decide to walk away. I promise you that I will not pester you anymore. I will continue to fight for my family and hope that I succeed. No hard feelings, no anger."

She raised two fingers in front of her face. "Scout's honor."

Maria fell silent, waiting for Marcus to reply. He felt his body had become one big washing machine in which his heart, stomach, and mind all flip-flopped and tumbled. He felt nauseous.

But his mind was made up, only now there was no chance of going back. He slowly raised Maria's hand to his lips, kissed it gently, and said, "Let's save your family."

CHAPTER 13

Marcus stared at the clock standing in a corner of the Garden Room, focusing on its metronome cadence. Maria had warned him the transition back could be rough, but since his soul was more attuned than most to the Otherworld, she didn't expect it to be difficult. Most likely she was trying to distract him, keep him from thinking too much about possibilities.

Regardless, his mind was reeling, trying to make sense of the entire day. If all went according to plan, maybe even best case, he could easily end up in a padded cell with saliva dribbling off his lips, talking to the walls in hopes of hearing something in return. He had witnessed it himself, where some coped with their internal disasters by adopting different voices to salvage their extraneous personalities.

Now he was questioning everything he thought he understood. Was it possible those *different* voices were actually other people occupying the same gray matter as their host? The concept gave him chills even while making a twisted sort of sense. It certainly was plausible. It could explain what was happening for some who struggled with mental health, too often summarily dismissed as 'just pull yourself up by the bootstraps and suck it up buttercup' types of therapy.

Some forms of mental instability could literally be a fracturing of the mind into jagged little pieces that felt like slivers under fingernails, meaning the problems that people faced were very real indeed.

Marcus had always looked at mental health with a sympathetic eye; he had seen plenty of good people suffering through depression, apathy, sadness, and that impending sense of doom when something was on its way but never quite arrived. It was a crippling affliction, but if there were evidence that outside forces were at work, at least in some cases, a new treatment possibility could be developed. It would be like finding a divining rod with instructions on the handle.

But for now, he needed to focus on the task at hand, to stay strong in order to take in the *Dark Man*; Craig. He shuddered in spite of his resolve.

Craig. The name was bugging him. There was a connection, ultimately an important one that he was unable to solder into the story to make all the circuits light up. It frustrated him.

Marcus equated the feeling with a muscle twitch that couldn't be rubbed out or the sensation of bugs crawling on skin. Someone mentions walking through a spiderweb, and suddenly it felt like spiders were crawling everywhere. That was this sensation, and it was wholly unpleasant.

Focus!

He shook his head to clear the thoughts and then looked over at Maria who was watching him from the corner.

He took a deep breath, held it, nodded his head, and exhaled fiercely. The universe went dark. Initially there was nothing. No sensation, no light, nothing, like a sensory deprivation tank. Then a tingle rising from his lower extremities. It felt like his legs were falling asleep, then his trunk, arms, and his face, and he tried to scream. But his body was sleeping. He couldn't wake up. A weight sat on his chest and pressed harder, slowly and inexorably crushing out his breath. He feared if he completely exhaled the heaviness would settle in his lungs, not allowing them to ever inflate with oxygen again. He panicked. He was dying! Had she tricked him? All this only to die?

And then he was moving. The weight released and in the distant inky dark a light shone. Or was it close and small? He couldn't tell. The empty space around him filled with fuzzy moving images not unlike the ones that can be seen out of the corner of the eye, squiggles and zigzags and protozoans. He was moving faster, speeding toward the light.

I am *dying*, he thought, as he clamped his eyes shut. It didn't help. If he opened his eyes, would he find himself on a bullet train into oblivion or rocket ship headed out of the earth's atmosphere?

Suddenly, the rushing sounds of water and waves bombarded him, surrounded, filled him, and then as instantly turned to static.

He broke through...something. He was on the other side. Without looking he saw himself as spirit; perfection outside of a broken, illogical human body. Peace like he had never experienced enveloped him, with joy to unending, and hope unrestricted.

And then that world caved in on itself like a series of Escher tiles, shifting and combining until forever absorbed into a single tile. When nothing existed apart from him but the singular, Marcus knew he could scrub through his history inside this tile; pause, rewind, slo-mo all at his disposal. But he had no time, moving past before he had a chance to reconcile himself to his history.

The momentum increased and Marcus could feel himself existing in and through eons of the universe, from the beginning of human time to present and into future. Everything merged together, nothing distinguishable, but he felt the emotions of every event within human understanding; pleasure, pain, suffering, sadness, joy, horror, elation, purity, anger, everything. He was full to bursting and for a moment thought it would happen; even his spirit would tear at the seams and the universe would be poisoned with his entrails, the sands of time contaminated with his detritus and his blood polluting the purity of universal waters.

Then empty! He was empty; nothing existed within him. He was a shell, a vessel to be controlled and manipulated at will. Id, ego, and superego gone and, in their place, nothing.

But it wasn't 'nothing.' He still existed somewhere or suspended lost in this nowhere. He was at least aware, somehow.

Then the 'nothing' began to enter his mind as if being sewn into his head by deep black threads with a razor-sharp needle. He felt the pinpricks, in and out, through and around, above and below. His entire sense of self couldn't escape the moving pinpricks now like spiders crawling over and through him. Again, he wanted to scream, but his voice had been stolen, detached from his body, and floating somewhere in the infinite.

His feet touched ground and he was running down a long corridor. Doors to his left and right opened and shut and he heard bits and pieces, more glimpses of his life, but from the perspective of this other place. Moments of misunderstanding that originated strife, sequences of events that led to long-lasting friendship, hatred barely under the surface kept hidden, betrayals of self and others.

Suddenly and unexpectedly there was a familiar hand, entwined with his. He looked around but couldn't find its source. Maria? Guiding him through this last section of the Otherworld, the central processing unit of the universe. He knew too, that he could choose to stay here, in the

Otherworld. Others had, and so could he. The Otherworld where darkness and light were not mutually exclusive but cohabited in a sick yin-yang of muddled ferocity. Where light bled into dark and dark invaded light to create a murky surface tension, and to break through was to be reborn, pushing through the mucus, coughing up the placenta of time and space.

But there was another presence here too, and opening his eyes he believed he could perceive it was the true form of God. Ferocious love! And the fires of this love burned in order to destroy the darkness that coursed through the soul of humanity, to cleanse the spirit, and to refine the clay into a vessel glazed with this deep, unending affection.

It was nothing he had ever felt, and everything he had ever hoped or longed for in the deep places where words were never sufficient. Finally, he was the son come home after slogging through pig muck, a lover returned after clarity is complete and fully restored, an equal welcomed with open arms and heart. In this space was invasive courage. Here, fairness was obliterated by loving justice. And grace, overlapping grace, unending grace embracing the whole of Alpha and Omega, from beginning to end. This was home. Here is where he wished to stay for all eternity, but he knew it was only a taste, a hint of what was to come.

And now he looked off into the distance and saw a pit. Though unwilling, it was his sight that carried there, to a place that held essences of dread, agony, and suffering. At its edge he could hear the screeches of a thousand eels roiling in the darkness, the echoes of bones bending and shattering in the struggle to find rest within the sinews of the darkness.

Then, he was moving above and held over the pit. Hopelessness pierced his soul; a sense of separation like an eternity without consciousness, a decision made within the soul to give up and be lost in the dark abyss of infinity.

His body was wracked with silent sobs because he knew there nothing else existed. He deserved to be thrown into this pit and crushed by the writhing snakes until he was no more. He wished for the death of his conscious mind, to lapse into non-being. More than anything he simply wanted an end. *The* end.

But no relief of an end. Instead, it felt like a film reel that was repeatedly spooled, withdrawing any hope of a final act. Hopelessness folded onto hopelessness, that singular tile. No hope, no even the power to escape in a suicide of the mind. No vegetating the brain to elude remembrance.

The pit ended, and Marcus's feet touched solid ground. He knew he had glimpsed heaven and been exposed to hell. Maria had chosen to forgo either infinite in order to protect her family.

His resolve was now set in Merlin's stone; the sword planted deep within the granite. He only had to remove the blade, seal his fate, and save a family. He hoped he would keep the memories of this place, existing as it did outside of space and time. If it were an internal memorial, it would be comfort enough. But then, he now knew it was all enough.

The sense of returning filled him so strongly that he knew his journey was about to end. Back to the 'real' world. He mentally gathered all the understanding he had gained, all the treasures and trauma, all the senses and experiences and put them in a special box in his mind. Maybe he would be able to open that box at any time to remind himself of the other side; the hope at the end of the prism.

He was now again in his mortal body. Odd, to feel so out of place within his own physical self. But his synapses were firing in their unique and deliberate sequences, and it only took a few moments to be at home once again.

He took a deep breath, followed by another. When he opened his eyes, he saw Maria sitting in front of him, talking and smiling, and he forgot everything he had witnessed; the experience stricken from the record.

CHAPTER 14

Marcus exhaled. He shook his head. It was Cynthia, not Maria, who was talking to him.

"—but I told my mom that there was no way he said that." Cynthia saw that Marcus was staring at her and smiling, she lowered her voice. "Welcome back. Is my mom with you?"

Tell her I am.

It startled him and he almost fell out of his chair. After his heart stopped jackhammering in his chest, he looked up, as if trying to look into his own head. "Geez, warn a guy."

Apologies.

He looked back at Cynthia and nodded. "Yeah, she's here with me. How long was I gone?"

Cynthia shrugged slightly. "I dunno. Ten minutes?"

Marcus shook his head, clearing the remaining cobwebs. "It felt like a lot longer than that. Like, most of a lifetime."

I told you time was different in the Otherworld.

Marcus nodded his head and smiled at Cynthia. "Well, thanks for covering for me. I imagine our time together was to give me time to talk to your mother. You are a strong, young girl, very brave protecting your brother. Now I need to talk to him. Would you please send him out here?"

Cynthia hopped off her chair and walked toward the house. "Of course."

Marcus sat, looking around the garage at all the random bits and pieces piled up on the shelves. Nothing jumped out to him as important. When Cynthia opened the door to the kitchen, she surprised her father, who acted like he hadn't been listening to their conversation. Regardless what he had done, he really did seem like a good father.

Told you.

Oh, so you can read my mind now? Marcus thought back.

Makes it easier to communicate without you arousing suspicion or looking like a crazy person.

True.

Marcus closed his eyes, suddenly feeling weary, as if something was trying to get him out of the house, and immediately. Probably Craig, which, if he was being honest, was about the worst name for a ghost, ever.

Agreed.

This is going to take some getting used to. Marcus took a deep breath and tapped his fingers against his knees rhythmically.

A moment later Charlie walked into the garage, over to him, and held out his hand. Marcus smiled and took the boy's hand, shaking it professionally.

"My dad said you are Mr. Grimm." Charlie seemed like the kind of kid who thought very carefully about everything. Any words out of his mouth would be calculated and well processed. That meant two things: First, Marcus could take almost everything Charlie said to the bank, and second, this conversation might take a while. But Marcus was looking more for clarification than answers to questions.

He gestured to the seat across from him. "Would you like to sit down?"

Charlie nodded and sat.

"Is it all right if I ask you some questions?"

"What kind of questions?" The boy's eyes glittered with intelligence; the same glimmer he had seen in his mother's eyes.

"I don't want to frighten you, but I need to ask you about the *Dark Man.*" Charlie shifted uncomfortably in his seat. His eyes scanned the room, making sure the *Dark Man* was nowhere around.

Charlie leaned forward and whispered, "Okay," before settling back in his seat and folding his hands in his lap.

"Is the *Dark Man* your uncle?" Marcus could feel that time was slipping in a much different cadence than in the Otherworld and every moment had a sense of urgency. He figured he needed to get the question out there quickly.

Just get right into it, Columbo. You want to ask my son if John poisoned me too?

Marcus smirked. *I think time is of the essence. That's all.*

Charlie eyed him curiously, and instead of answering the question asked one of his own. "Who are you talking to?"

The question was so unexpected that Marcus floundered for a response. He cleared his throat and said, "Your mom."

Charlie nodded. "I thought so." Marcus watched the boy physically relax. His mother's presence put him at ease. This would help.

Something about mothers put children at ease. Of course, there were exceptions, but they only proved the rule. The maternal instinct transcended the boundaries of science. It made sense that there was a psychic connection between the one that carried a child within them, and then fed them with their own body after birth. It was akin to going through a great distress, which birth most often is, and syncing one's thought and emotional patterns with the other. Children tend to be empathetic by nature, but there was that extra step and bond between mother and child.

Science couldn't explain a mother's ability to lift an immovable object to save her child. Sure, science might justify it as adrenaline, but there is more to it than that. It wasn't as if a mother had time to find and take a drug, like PCP, wait for it to kick in, and then save their child. Of course, the synapses fired in the brain sending hormones to the right sections in order to enhance ability, but that simplistic explanation wasn't enough. Sometimes 'unexplainable' and 'wonder full' is the best explanation.

Charlie was staring intently, and Marcus quickly brought himself back. "Can we talk about the *Dark Man*?"

Again, Charlie shifted uneasily, but this time he settled quickly and nodded his head.

"He is my Uncle Craig. I don't think he likes me." Marcus noticed that Charlie shrank into himself as he spoke about his uncle. He could also feel Maria shifting uncomfortably in his mind. She didn't like seeing her son like this, and Marcus couldn't blame her, but he was certain she wouldn't stop the questions, knowing they were important.

"Why would you say that?" As Marcus asked the question, Charlie drew his leg up toward him and clutched the ankle where he had seen the mark earlier that day.

"I see. Has he hurt you before?"

"He tried, but my mom stopped him." Marcus felt a flame burn through his body. Maria was fuming, and rightfully so.

"How do you know it was your mom that stopped him? Maybe you stopped him." Marcus was trying to be gentle with the questions, but he knew that shortly he would have to ask something that would test Maria's ability to remain detached during this process. He gently reminded her that it was paramount she remain calm and objective in order to save her children. He didn't feel a response.

"No. It was my mom. Cynthia told me. Cynthia never lies to me." He sat up straighter, proud of himself for supporting his sister.

"I have no doubt. She loves you very much too. You're her favorite brother." Marcus let the corner of his mouth rise ever so slightly to make sure Charlie was in on the joke.

He needn't have worried. Charlie giggled and said as only a four-year-old is able, "That's cause I'm her *only* brother."

As quickly, Charlie's face lost its good humor and looked on the verge of crying. Marcus marveled at the shift in emotions, the complexity behind them. If he had been exposed to what Charlie had been at this age, he might have developed a little complexity himself.

"Can I tell you something, Mr. Grimm? Something I don't want my mom to hear."

Marcus considered the request. He didn't want to lie to the boy, and he wanted to be respectful at the same time. So, he compromised.

"I don't think I can make your mom not listen. That's not up to me, Charlie. Besides, I'm fairly certain she will want to hear anything you have to say."

Charlie frowned, then taking a deep breath whispered, "I can't remember what she looks like. My mom."

Marcus felt a shudder so intense he himself almost burst into tears. Academically, assuming there was an Academy for the study of an entity cohabiting one's mind, he knew the emotions were from Maria. But emotionally it felt like the feelings were his. It was an amazingly confusing paradox he wasn't sure he would ever get used to but could live with if he must.

That triggered a thought about Craig, and the intensity he felt about everything. No wonder Maria said they would need to work together. Marcus now understood better its importance.

Marcus felt Maria relax, so he took it as permission to continue. "Your dad has pictures of her."

Charlie shrugged. "Only in his bedroom, and he doesn't allow us to go in there."

John hadn't removed the Pentagram from under the carpet, simply covered it up. He remembered the newer carpet he had seen in the bedroom earlier. Understandably, John didn't want his kids anywhere near it but didn't dare scrub it away either.

He's afraid that if he gets rid of it, his brother will go with it, or...might never go.

Marcus nodded. Charlie cocked his head to one side, giving the impression of a curious pigeon. "Maybe you could ask him sometime if you could see the picture."

Charlie nodded and sniffed. Marcus saw tears edging in, threatening to slide down his cheeks and changed the subject. "Do you have a favorite toy?"

Charlie's eyes lit up and a small smile played at the edges of his lips. "My dinosaur. His name is Michael. He's a Velociraptor. He keeps me safe from the bad man."

In an instant Charlie went from happy to shut down. His countenance darkened and his eyes shifted around the garage, as if waiting for someone to reprimand him. Or hurt him.

Marcus let him sit in the paranoia for a moment and then leaned forward. "The *Dark Man*? Your uncle?"

Charlie also leaned forward. Their faces were inches away from each other and Marcus hoped John wouldn't show up at this moment to check on what was happening.

When Charlie spoke, it was in a whisper with a finger to his lips. "Shhh. If he knows we're talking about him, he'll come." He hesitated, "He told me he wants to watch you suffer. That watching you suffer will give him strength."

Marcus glanced around the room and then back to Charlie. "What else did your uncle say?"

Charlie furrowed his brow and looked at Marcus with a puzzled look on his face. "He said something I don't know."

"Do you want to try and tell me?"

Charlie shrugged. "He said that when he is done with you, he is going to pack you with your own brick? I don't think he meant that, but it sounded like that."

I can't wait to get ahold of him.

Marcus felt his pulse quicken. The fact that Craig was speaking to a young child in this manner didn't instill any confidence in his character. That tickle returned to the back of his mind, but still the truth associated remained elusive.

"Well Charlie, your uncle shouldn't be saying those kinds of things to you. They are unkind, and I'm sorry he said them."

"What does it mean?"

Marcus stuttered around the words for a split second before responding, "I think maybe you should ask your dad. He might be able to tell you."

Charlie nodded. "Okay."

Marcus and Maria let out a sigh of relief simultaneously, and Marcus wondered what else he might get from Charlie. He was four years old, and his world was basically TV and toys, as most normal four-year-olds would want for their life. That age should be full of uninhibited play, of not worrying about the greater expanse of the universe, not having to figure out what was for dinner or what the plans were for the next day. To be four was to wonder when you could play next and trying to plead your way into a later bedtime. Simple and easy. Marcus envied the innocence of youth and its raw ability to believe the unbelievable, with an almost scientific aptitude.

But Charlie *was* four years old and right at the center of this chaos. And he needed help, along with his sister and parents. They needed to be free of Uncle Craig and his penchant for hurting his nephew and being uninhibitedly crass.

Although, Marcus wanted to end this quickly, he knew he wasn't fully ready. He didn't have the complete picture. There were a few edge pieces still missing, and one very crucial center piece. Whatever that was would unravel the entire mystery of why he was here and what precisely he was supposed to do about it.

Marcus stared at Charlie for a few seconds. It was amazing how someone could be resilient enough to smile one second and conspiratorial the next. It was almost eerie, unsettling.

It also spoke to an elasticity of a child's mind that disappeared with age. The rubber band theory of a child versus an adult was one that had always intrigued Marcus and made the most sense. If you thought of age as a rubber band, for a child it is fresh, elastic, and returns to its natural state easily and quickly. But as one ages, the band loses its elasticity and becomes more rigid. Instead of returning to its original resilience it gets weaker and stretches. The further a child gets from that innocence, the more brittle the band becomes. A child may experience trauma but is often able to separate and bounce back.

Someone in their 40s or 50s experiencing the same no longer has that ability and it cracks their mind. The entropy of the universe is a relentless disintegration that humans resist as long as possible. Inevitably, it wins, and humanity returns to the earth, ashes to ashes.

Marcus had no doubt that Charlie could recover from what was happening as long as it didn't continue for much longer. Repeated and prolonged stressors aged a rubber band prematurely, no matter how elastic it was at the beginning. It infuriated him that Charlie was being exposed to the type of stressor that could alter his mental course, all because his father couldn't let go of his brother.

With tears forming at the corners of his eyes, Marcus turned back to Charlie and asked, "Do you want your Uncle Craig to be gone for good?"

Charlie started to nod and then all the color ran from his face. He gripped the armrests so intensely, his knuckles turned white-blue with the effort.

My sweet boy Maria wailed in a desperate voice, and Marcus felt himself propelled toward Charlie. He couldn't have stopped himself if he wanted. Maria was incredibly strong.

His next thought was wholly his own. *I am incredibly glad you are on my side.*

He was kneeling in front of Charlie, holding his hands out in case he needed to steady him. "What is it Charlie?"

It took Charlie a moment, but when he looked up there was pure terror in his eyes. "He knows. He knows we've been talking about him."

Now it was Marcus's face that went slack. Then came the rattling from the back-garage door leading into the yard. Marcus looked up, startled, and saw the doorknob violently shaking. For a brief moment, he imagined he saw an apparition, Craig, hovering right behind the door, unable to actually enter and could feel the rage. Then it was gone. As simple as that. The darkness left the garage and neutrality returned.

Marcus heard a strange sucking sound and realized Charlie was hyperventilating. He couldn't decide if the panic that was rising was in his own mind or Maria's. He scanned the garage for a paper bag to help Charlie breathe but there wasn't one. So, he firmly placed both hands on the boy's shoulders and looked into his eyes.

"Charlie, I need you to try and take a big breath in through your nose and out through your mouth. Force the air to leave your body. Breathe deep and slow. Can you do that for me?"

Marcus could sense Maria pacing back and forth in his mind. It was disorienting and made him a bit nauseous.

Maria, I need you to stop worrying and let me handle this. If you continue to pace, I won't be able to focus, and your boy is going to pass out.

Instantly, it stopped, and Marcus was better able to concentrate. Charlie was doing his best to obey the instructions. Every time he drew in a breath, he made an exaggerated face, as if he were trying to suck all the air out of the universe, and when he exhaled his mouth became a comical 'O' until all the air exited his lungs. Marcus nodded encouragement and the process repeated for about a minute. The color returned to Charlie's face and his knuckles released the chair. There were indentations where the fingers met the palm of Charlie's hand, accentuating how tightly the boy had been holding on.

They sat there until Charlie was fully under control, and then Marcus squeezed his shoulders.

"Charlie, you are a very brave boy. I think that's it. We don't need to talk anymore about the *Dark Man*, okay?"

Charlie nodded and wiped his eyes; he looked absolutely drained. If

Marcus had been wavering at all about his part in this situation, his resolve was now rock solid. If he didn't remove Craig from this house in one way or another, this family was going to lose more family members, and soon.

Marcus stood up and dusted off his knees. He gestured toward the house and Charlie went without a word.

As Marcus turned to follow Charlie, Maria gave instructions. *Marcus, I want you to separate yourself from the family. Tell John you need to get a last sense of the house and yard before you can finish your assessment.*

Marcus nodded and opened the door to the kitchen.

CHAPTER 15

They entered the kitchen. John was standing by the stove, stirring a cup of tea with a small spoon. He looked up expectantly, and with a father's instinct, knew something had happened in the garage. He moved to his son and embraced him.

"Are you okay? What did he do?"

The boy sniffed and shook his head. "Nothing. I'm okay. Can I go watch cartoons?"

John held him at arm's length, making sure he wasn't hiding anything.

"Of course you can, buddy. Your sister is in there. Go snuggle up next to her."

Charlie moved off to the living room, still sniffing slightly, but still looking apprehensive.

John stood up and glared at Marcus. Marcus took the glare and said nothing. John walked over to him and poked a finger into his chest.

"I swear to God, if I find out you harassed my boy or hurt him in any way, I will sue you and you will never work another day in your life."

Marcus opened his mouth to reply, "I would expect…

Maria knew where he was headed and cut him off: *You can't say that to him right now. He doesn't know you know it's his brother.*

Marcus's words changed mid-sentence, "…nothing less of you as his father. That's why I want to help you."

John's finger dropped and he looked down at the floor, as if conflicted.

There it was again, that tingle of an itch at the back of his brain that had been annoying Marcus. But, still nothing solid as to what it was. An itch that couldn't be scratched.

He smiled at John. "I need to walk the property inside and out one last time by myself in order to get my last impressions. Would that be all right?"

John stared at him for a long moment, as if he were consulting a board of directors in his head for a final approval.

Finally, he sighed and replied simply, "Yeah, that's fine. I'll be in the living room with the kids if you need anything. Okay?"

Marcus nodded and John turning, walked toward the living room.

"Oh, John. You forgot your tea. You might want to take that with you."

John looked back, almost apologetically, "Oh, the tea. I brewed that for you. Thought it might help settle some nerves as you wander our house."

There was nothing sinister in the way John said it, but it was all wrong and instantly another piece of the puzzle fell into place.

John means to follow through and kill me for his brother.

Maria didn't respond verbally, but Marcus knew she agreed. He would take the cup with him on his rounds, and once he was in a spot where John wouldn't notice, he would dump out the tea. And then he would wait to see John's reaction when he didn't get sleepy…or fall down dead. *Thank you very much and a nice day to you too.*

"Thank you, John, that is kind." John smiled and nodded, turning to go to his children as Marcus picked up the cup. He stirred the tea with the spoon and then placed it gently in the sink.

Where to first, boss? he asked without speaking.

First, there is a crawl space inside the hall closet. I need you to go down there and find a box. Don't worry, there is plenty of space. I wouldn't really even call it a crawl space. It's more like a tiny basement.

Maria chuckled, which brought a smile to Marcus's face. He wasn't certain whether the emotion was his or hers, or perhaps, both. One thing was certain, if this union continued, he might never again be able to accurately assess which emotions were truly his own. With only one person inside him he already felt fractured: not quite whole.

Marcus began to walk through the living room toward the hall. *Don't go immediately there. John is on edge. He has made up his mind to get rid of you, so he is going to be wary of anything that seems odd.*

Instead of heading for the hall closet, as he originally intended, Marcus entered Cynthia's room. He didn't expect to feel anything different, but as he stepped inside emotions increased. Because Maria was now a part of him, he felt a flow of energy and love strong enough to almost buckle his knees. He grabbed onto the door frame to steady himself, took a deep breath, and stepped further inside.

Flashes of Cynthia as a baby played like a slide show in his head. Here she was lying in a bassinette, looking up at her mom. Another image of her taking her first steps. Another where she had scraped her knee and was crying. Her mom wiped away the tears with a sleeve of her sweater. The last one was Cynthia looking at her mother, lying in bed. It must have been when Maria was sick, and the role of caretaker had somewhat reversed. Cynthia held out a cup of tea. The picture abruptly stopped as Marcus put more pieces together. He was certain the rage he felt rising in him was his own and was about to ask.

She didn't know. She just thought she was bringing me a cup of tea. Marcus's legs felt weak.

How could he? How dare he? What a coward!

Marcus was yelling into his own mind and Maria didn't seem to have an answer for him.

Then another question: *Why didn't you stop drinking the tea when you knew you were being poisoned?* A heavy silence followed his query, and Marcus felt shame fill the emptiness.

Maria's response was slow and sad. *I thought that maybe he was right. Maybe the cancer was there to stay. And that it might be nice to end it on my terms, instead of being in pain for however long it took the cancer to destroy my body. He was wrong. I was wrong.*

Marcus could feel his anger now mixing with something else: grief. This was compassion and it had nowhere to go. His logic wanted to argue the sanctity of life, the keeping of hope until the last possible moment, but he couldn't. He had never been in her situation, and he didn't know what he would have done if he were facing the same difficult circumstances. He hoped he would make a different decision but speculating and judging would be hurtful and unfair.

Instead, he focused on what truly wasn't fair, and what he hoped little would never know.

He knew what he was doing, and he used his little girl to accomplish it. That makes him a coward.

Silence, and then, *I wish I could argue with but I can't. That was terribly wrong.*

Marcus felt her leave. She disappeared. Perhaps she had gone to her Garden Room to be alone, which was all right. With her withdrawal,

Marcus understood that what he was now thinking and feeling was actually his and not originating from her. He needed that clarity to figure things out.

He wondered if perhaps Maria had stayed behind rather than crossing over, in part because of her own shame; the need to atone for her sins in some way.

He stood in the doorway for a few more seconds and then figured it was time to head to the crawl space. Reaching the hall closet, he paused to see if he was visible from the living room and was dismayed to find that he could indeed be seen for a brief moment. As quietly as possible, he entered the closet and closed the door behind him, hoping that John hadn't spotted.

Marcus stood with his forehead against the door for a long moment, listening for any sudden movements or sounds. When he was satisfied, he felt along the wall and found a light switch. He moved to the trap door set into the floor near the back and grabbing the giant metal handle, tugged. The door was far heavier than he anticipated, and it slipped from his fingers banging down into its spot.

Marcus winced at the sound and stood perfectly still for a few seconds, his heart thumping in his chest, before bracing himself and trying again. This time the door groaned up onto its hinges and insulation floated down onto the carpet. He dipped his head into the hole and saw a pull string, which turned on another light. As Maria had indicated, the space was more a small room than a crawlspace.

Marcus climbed in and down the ladder, making sure to close the hatch behind him. The odor was musty, nothing unexpected for a crawl space or basement. He smiled at himself realizing that with all the craziness of the day he had half expected to smell a rotting corpse down here.

As his eyes adjusted, he searched the space. Boxes with the word *Christmas* on them were stacked along one wall, a few old heirlooms scattered about, and not much else other than accumulated household detritus. Now he wished Maria hadn't taken a sabbatical. He needed her help.

Marcus set his tea down by one of the big boxes, and began rifling through the contents, searching for anything that might give him some new clue to make sense of this oddity of a day. Box after box there was nothing that seemed relevant. No special knick-knacks or curious; nothing that drew attention in any meaningful way.

He was beginning to question Maria's motives for having him search here at all when he noticed scuff marks on the floor behind an old trunk. They were barely visible, the dust having nearly buried them. Tucked in the darkest corner was a medium sized non-descript box with no markings, like a filing box, but bigger. With some effort, Marcus dragged it out and slid it across the floor until he was sitting on the bottom rung of the ladder with the box in front of him. He lifted the lid.

Inside were letters, mementos, and lots of pictures. It appeared to be full of special items, the sort of treasures kept by a husband and wife. He rifled through a few of the letters but returned them without opening. He doubted the clues he was looking for would be hidden in love notes between the married couple.

He picked up a stack of photos and began browsing. Most were of John, Maria, and their children in various settings: going on vacation, hanging out around the house, school pictures, family celebrations and the like. Nothing significant.

He reached for another stack and found they were stuck together. Slowly and carefully he pried them apart, the sound like skin peeling away from muscle. Once separated, he began looking through them. Besides the core family of four, there was another person in the photos and in some a boy appeared with the stranger, standing near but appearing uncomfortable. A few photos and again the boy, standing near the stranger looking awkward.

Marcus surmised the unknown adult was probably Craig. Maybe the boy was Craig's son? He didn't know if Craig had a son, but he couldn't think of any other reason for his appearance in family pictures.

Marcus looked closer. The boy not only looked uncomfortable, he looked scared. And something else...

And then it hit him. Marcus recognized exactly who the boy was and instantly knew the connection. He now understood why Craig wanted him dead and why this whole day was far more significant than he could have imagined.

When he had examined the photo, he saw it. A slight staining around one of the boy's wrists. He almost dismissed it as a smudge created when he separated the photos, but when he rubbed it with his finger trying to remove it, he realized the discoloration was part of the original.

Marcus felt sick to his stomach and his head began to swim. He was so focused on the photo and what it revealed that he didn't hear the soft *whump* of something hitting the floor above his head.

He looked at the older man in the photo again and his memory confirmed what he saw; this was the man he had called the police to arrest, the man later murdered in his jail cell while the guards looked the other way. And here too was his son, orphaned when his dad was taken away and killed.

How had he not seen it? How had he been so blind? He sat back against the ladder trying to process his shock.

Now he understood. John knew who he was this entire time. He never had any intention of ousting his brother from the house. It was all a ruse, one perpetrated to some extent by Maria. She had said she was the one that made it all happen; she was the one that made sure Marcus came to the house. That meant she had known this entire time and had said nothing.

Worse, she had told Marcus that there were things he needed to discover for himself, which he did, but only after he signed away his rights as an independent in this tragedy. Once he was in for a pound, once he was committed to the gamble, once there was no way out, then he could know that the spirit he was dealing with was the pedophile he had sent away over a year ago. No wonder Craig was so pissed off! Now he needed to be even more careful; John most certainly *was* watching his every move.

Marcus stood up, dusted off his butt, put the photos back in the box, replaced the lid, and slid the box back into its corner. Hopefully, this would long be over before John discovered that he had tampered with anything sensitive.

Satisfied that everything looked normal, he headed up the ladder and pushed on the trap door. It didn't move. Something was holding the door down from above. He tried twice more, pushing harder, but only managed to budge the door about half an inch before the weight was too much.

Marcus dropped back down into the crawl space and sat down. Obviously, something was on top of the door, but he couldn't recall anything in the closet that was heavy or precarious enough to do that. Maybe, Craig had tipped something over in hopes of trapping him here, only to be discovered long after he was dead.

But, as Marcus thought about his predicament, the most likely scenario was that John had discovered he had gone down into the crawl space and had blocked him in here. Panic hadn't quite settled in Marcus's chest, but it was trying to breach the perimeter and the adrenaline was making him slightly dizzy.

Instead of giving in to his emotions, he set his mind to work. First, he pushed all the boxes back where they had originally been, as close as he could remember. He stood back and looked at his work, pleased but still skittish. Using his hands, he next swept the dust around, trying to make it look natural, as if he had simply circled the room looking at, but not touching anything.

When he was satisfied, he clapped and rubbed his hands together to get rid of most of the dust and climbed the ladder again. This time he banged on the underside of the door and yelled as loudly as he was able.

"Hey! I think something fell on top of the door! Can someone help me?" He yelled it repeatedly, until he finally heard the sound of shuffling feet above him, followed by the muffled efforts of someone moving something heavy. Finally, the door lifted, and John was standing there, the look on his face wavering between disbelief and suspicion, maybe even disappointment. Marcus tried to neutralize his own expressions or to at least look grateful.

"Whew!" he exclaimed. "That was a little unnerving."

Turn the light off. Maria's voice returned so unexpectedly that Marcus flinched.

Welcome back, he shot back at the voice as he reached for the string.

Turning off the light he reached up and accepted John's outstretched hand.

"I think this old punching bag must've fallen and trapped you down there. I'm so sorry. That could have been horrible."

Every word out of John's mouth now felt false. Nothing he said could be trusted any more. But Marcus maintained his composure.

"Well, I'm glad you heard me pounding and yelling or it could have been a long night." He even mustered a smile.

John pointed at Marcus's face. "Are you okay? You seem a little flustered. Do you feel ill?"

Marcus wiped his forehead with the back of his hand and thought, *oh no, I left the tea down there.*

Play it up, he heard Maria. *Act like you're feeling sick. Put him at ease.*

Still looking at John, Marcus allowed his eyes to flutter a bit and his balance to waver, and he said, "You know? Maybe it's my claustrophobia kicking in, but I do feel a little dizzy and nauseous."

John nodded his head, concerned. His eyes flicked to the dark crawl space and then back to Marcus.

"What were you doing down there, anyhow? We didn't go down there before. Did you feel something? A presence?"

With what he now knew, it seemed that every word out of John's mouth was a lie, an act intended to deceive. But Marcus showed none of this on his face.

"I just wanted to be absolutely thorough. There was nothing down there that was helpful."

Veiled relief flitted across John's face, but the suspicion still hung in at the corners of his eyes.

"That's too bad. I wish we could finally get some answers. Maybe you should sit down a bit? Take a breather; get your bearings back."

Marcus shook his head, both as a response and as a way to show that he was clearing the cobwebs from his brain.

"I'll be all right. I would like to finish sooner than later if you don't mind. You go back with your kids in the living room and I will let you know when I am ready to give you a rundown of everything I have discovered and the next steps we need to take." He laid on his most sincere smile and patted John on the shoulder.

John appeared hesitant to leave and Marcus could almost see the wheels turning in his head. If he insisted on staying with Marcus it would seem suspicious. Quickly, he made his decision.

"Okay, that sounds fine to me. Just holler again if you need anything else. Are you sure you're okay?"

Marcus smiled and nodded. "Long day. It shouldn't take much longer." He faked a burp. John, seemingly satisfied, turned and left, heading back toward the living room and his recliner.

Marcus shook his head and, relieved, laughed to himself. Maria chuckled.

"Okay, so now where are we going?" Marcus asked out loud before realizing he had even spoken.

I need to take you out to the shed in the backyard.

Marcus nodded. *Tallyho, let's go!* Every nerve in his body was still giddy with adrenaline and he snickered to himself again before leaving the closet.

CHAPTER 16

Marcus strode through the backyard, taking deep sips of fresh air through his nose, releasing the carbon dioxide out through his mouth. His mind was still reeling from the previous fifteen minutes. If he didn't know unequivocally that he had left the full teacup in the crawl space, he may have thought he *had* been poisoned. The aftermath of the 'rush'.

The shed looked smaller than he remembered, and he hesitated for a moment. He hadn't ever been prone to claustrophobia, but once stated, even as a lie, it seemed possible, almost a way of speaking unconscious awareness into experience.

He pulled on the handle and the door grudgingly opened, releasing the smells of old grass caught in the belly of a lawnmower, dried weeds remnants stuck to a weed eater, and the general decay of earth. Once inside, he turned on the light and again saw the order. Now, it screamed of someone trying to occupy their mind to avoid less savory thoughts. Not a single tool or implement was out of place or crooked or missing; everything in its place and a place for everything.

Marcus moved to the center of the shed and stood over the drain. He looked down and bent to investigate, thinking maybe what he was looking for might be hidden down there. Maria brought him back quickly.

You could ask. It's not down there. How stupid would I be to hide the money down a drain?

Marcus felt color creep into his face, but smiled and shrugged his shoulders.

"So, somewhere in here is where the money is, huh?" he asked nonchalantly. Truthfully, he wasn't overly interested or motivated by the thought of money, no matter how much or little. But, he *was* curious as to how much Maria had been able to sock away.

Don't get all tight in the britches. If you turn around you will find a small, discolored panel behind the back bench in the shed. Pry that open. The money is in there.

"It can't really be *that* easy, can it?" Even as he asked, Marcus knew this was one of those superstitious rhetorical questions the universe was waiting for someone dumb enough to ask.

He grabbed a crowbar off its hook and approached the panel set low and into the back of the shed. As soon as he placed metal to metal, Marcus felt a surge of high voltage electricity enter his body, as though he had fallen victim to the world's biggest party buzzer. There was nothing pleasant about it. He fell back into the bench, grounding himself, and let go of the crowbar. It was a miracle he was alive. Usually, such a current would cause muscles to tighten and one couldn't let go of the instrument of pain and death.

His entire body tingled like a million tiny ants were crawling all over him. He tried to scratch them away, but the sensation remained. There was nothing to do but ride it out and hope it hadn't done any irreparable damage to his heart. The only response he got from Maria was *well, that's new.*

"Gee thanks." He checked his hair to make sure it wasn't standing on end and hoped that smoke wasn't coming out of his ears. "So, what do we do now?"

You got me. The answer was about what Marcus expected, but he could still feel her thinking, processing. Looking around the shed, he searched for something, anything, that might help him and found a breaker box hiding in a corner where the light almost didn't reach.

"Look!" he exclaimed and when he felt her turn, he experienced a moment of vertigo.

What are you waiting for? Go flip the switch.

He heard her speak, but his intuition told him that once he tripped that breaker something was going to happen, and not a good something. He had a growing sense of dread; that something was in the dark corners of the shed. It was undeniably powerful and growing, and Marcus felt it wash over his body.

Reluctantly, he walked up to the small breaker box, opened it, saw the single switch, and rested his finger on it. His whole body had broken out in a cold sweat. Something was desperately wrong, but he didn't know what. Before he could stop her, Maria reached out and flipped the switch for him. The shed plunged into darkness, blotting out the light that should have been coming through the solitary window. And then all hell broke loose.

First, came the whispers filling Marcus's internal world with hopelessness. Then, prickling sensations, as if his brain were being experimented on. Unknown words in a foreign language, perhaps not even of this realm, bombarded him from every side. He couldn't understand what they were saying, but the words filled him with trepidation.

Next, he felt a presence directly behind him. It leaned in and made a snuffling sound, as if it were trying to sniff out Marcus's essence, as if it were attempting to determine allegiances. The presence exhaled and Marcus dry heaved at the stench of rotting flesh. He dared not turn around but began to shiver uncontrollably. This was the darkest spirit he had ever encountered, a demon perhaps? The one that gifted him with its powers of discernment. It spoke, just above a whisper, but when it did, Marcus fell to his knees, weeping uncontrollably.

"This is not your place, Marcus Grimm. You do not belong here." A deep inhalation that sounded like a million souls screaming in unison. Marcus gave way and flopped fully to the ground, his face on the cement.

"Your soul is worth nothing. You are worth nothing. Speak and let me hear your voice. Give me your voice. It belongs to me now."

Still Marcus wept. He could feel tears streaming down his face and wondered if he would break in half. The demon bent over and breathed in his left ear. Marcus wanted to claw his ear out, wanted to make it all stop, but he couldn't move.

"Speak! Now!"

Marcus mumbled something, wondering where Maria was. Maybe she wasn't allowed in this place. Maybe she was afraid and left to protect her Garden Room. Regardless, Marcus knew he was completely alone. He cleared his throat and squeaked out a barely audible reply.

"You have no authority to take my voice."

The screeching entities in the room swirled faster, making Marcus's head spin crazily. He closed his eyes against the dark and tried to breathe calmly, but he was losing the battle. His body didn't want to cooperate, and his voice was trying to abandon ship.

"Your parents gave your voice over to me when you were a wee babe suckling at

the breast of your mother. Your voice has always been mine. Now speak it so I may claim you fully as my ward."

Marcus realized that he could speak inside his head without using his physical voice and the demon would still hear.

You would want and claim dominion over an infant child whose only instinct is to feed and sleep? The mind and soul of that child is not the same as the one inside the man that lay prostrate before you. You have no right to claim my voice. It is a different voice than the one that only knew how to coo or cry.

In between the spiraling loops of darkness that wound its way ever deeper into him, a thought occurred.

You are a false prophet.

The entity moved away quickly, as if he had been struck by a heavy object. The others in the room swirled faster and faster, raising a cacophony of sound that reminded Marcus very much of wind inside a tornado. They were frenzied, which caused the one behind him, the chief, to become confused. It needed order to be able to control, and its horde was not cooperating.

Marcus could wound them, but he needed the right sequence to destroy them. There was a truth within this space that needed to be spoken aloud, but the rising din in his mind prevented him from seeing what it was. And he hoped to God he could figure it out before it destroyed him.

You are not the demon that is a part of me. I have spoken to that one and we are entwined. It is inescapable. And you are not him.

Marcus felt a weight on his back and imagined that an incorporeal foot was on his back, grinding him into the floor.

How long have you dwelt in this place, demon? The interloper relaxed the pressure enough for Marcus to draw in a deep breath, which he instantly regretted, because the air tasted of death and decay.

"*This is of no concern to you. All that matters to you is that you give to me your voice. I claimed dominion over your voice on our first meeting, but you escaped my grasp. I will not allow that to happen again. Your voice, it belongs to me, now give it over.*"

Another deep inhalation of air, and as rotten as it was, Marcus's head cleared a little and he was able to think through the darkness.

Now it sounded like the creature was whining. Marcus knew it was trying to assert its terror and dominion over him, but all he heard in everything spoken was petulant sniveling. He half expected to hear, *come on guy, I really want it,* and Marcus laughed out loud, which sent the lesser fiends spiraling out of control again.

Marcus processed quickly all the demon had said, and that's when he felt fingers penetrating his mind. Unlike before, the sensation was instantly painful, like a hundred red hot pokers inserted into his cranium. there was no other way to describe it. He screamed in his head:

You have no permission here! You are not allowed inside my head! Get out!

But the fingers kept digging and Marcus felt himself losing consciousness. He tried to shake his head to clear it, but that only made the world tilt crazily. He vomited and blood vessels burst in his eyes. There was nothing to do but succumb to inevitable death.

Then a thought flickered. Maybe, what the demon said didn't matter, but what *he* already said did. What had he said?

His head swam and his buzzed with the sound of a million mosquitoes. And then it came to him.

You are *a false prophet.* The fingers hesitated.

Yeah. You are *a false prophet, because…* His head hurt; thinking hurt; everything hurt. …*because…* and everything clicked. He rolled over, looked the creature directly in its eye, or orifice, and spoke the words that released him from its grip.

"You are a false prophet because you are not Amdusias. As I said, you are *not* the one who inhabits my body. You want to claim me as your own and destroy my bond with Amdusias."

The demon started to back away, and Marcus was grateful. Simply looking at the creature made him want to claw his eyes out. He realized that his own hands were slowly making their way toward his face and he willed them back to his sides.

"Therefore, you have no authority over me, and I command you to leave. Remove your presence from this holy place. You do not belong here; you are not given permission to dwell here any longer."

Marcus was now fully standing and moved forward until his face was inches away from the demon's. He was full of resolve and as he smiled, he ended it.

"You and your horde do not belong here. So, you can kindly make your way back to the putrid hole in hell you crawled out of."

The swirling reached a fever pitch and everything in the shed rattled, tools falling to the ground, the panel shaking loose and clattering to the concrete. And just like that the shed was silent and empty. Marcus breathed in and out, afraid he was going to pass out.

Two thoughts crossed his mind: *Craig had been amassing an army. He didn't want John to kill me; he wanted to watch me suffer.*

The second thought that came on the heels of the first: *Craig is not going to appreciate it when he finds out I disbanded his misfits.*

Marcus felt Maria return.

Have a nice trip? he thought.

Maria stayed silent.

"Well," he stated, "I think the shed shook and loosened the panel in the wall. So, let's get what we came for and get out of here before I vomit again."

Agreed. Maria's voice sounded faint and frightened.

"Are you okay?" Marcus asked with genuine concern in his voice.

They tried to come into my Garden Room. They did their damnedest, but I think whatever you were saying to their leader was distracting enough so they didn't have the power to do any real damage. They looked horrid, purple blood dripping down their chins. Let's end this. Please. He felt her shudder.

"Gladly," Marcus replied. He walked over to the panel, pulled it easily away from the wall, and reached in. Initially he felt nothing, but reaching further in, felt the rough edges of a burlap sack. He pulled it out and then carefully in the dim light found his way to the breaker box. Without thinking, he flipped the switch and immediately heard the fizz and spark of the live wire dancing on the metal panel.

Opening the sack, Marcus looked inside.

One hundred and twenty-four thousand, four hundred and forty-four dollars, Maria told him.

"Okay then," was all he could say. It was much more than he had imagined.

Marcus flipped the breaker again sending the shed into darkness. This time the shed remained silent. It was simply a dark shed with light coming through the single window set into one of the walls.

"I would like to get out of here and move on to phase three, please," he whispered.

Couldn't agree more. Let's head to the bedroom and tie this all up with a neat little bow.

Marcus nodded, checked his hair again, and then walked out of the shed with the bag. His mind was still swirling, but his resolve would not waver, not this deep into the maze. He was ready to end it and be done with it all. Yet, at the same time, he knew that as soon as this part ended, the next part would begin, most likely in an asylum.

Just in case, he stopped by his car. He found his notepad, jotted a quick note, tore off the piece of paper, and slipped it into the burlap sack before throwing it into the trunk. The signed note simply said, *For my son.*

CHAPTER 17

As Marcus made his way back inside the house, he marveled at how life twisted and turned. As a baby he was forced into a gift that had made him money and helped people out, but it meant that on some level he was inhabited by a demon; apparently a fairly demure demon who was perfectly happy with Marcus going through life unaware and super powered. Although Marcus imagined he wasn't the only one the demon inhabited; he didn't know how space-time worked in the demon realm, but he was fairly certain it was different than Earth space-time. Also, he was reasonably sure he would have to pay with his soul or something along those lines when he died. He could argue until his face turned blue about how he was a baby when it happened, but he knew that demons really didn't give two craps unless it served their purposes, which meant losing a soul to the other side wasn't, in fact, a win.

And now, here he was, already entwined with one spirit, about to entangle with another, and he was willingly going along with it. The absurdity of life certainly had its moments. And he felt the end game coming. It was that ominous paranoia of someone always watching, waiting, ready to pounce. It was the sudden intake of breath before the gun shot. It was the unnatural calm in the eye of a hurricane. But he thought that maybe he was ready for it now. And at the end of it all, he would look John directly in the eyes and say, "Thank you and a nice day to you too."

He skirted the living room as best he could, hoping John would be too involved in his own thoughts to ask any questions. As he passed through the room, he held his stomach and grimaced as though his stomach were really starting to bother him. Unfortunately, John's paranoia didn't allow him to remain silent. "You about done? I need to feed the kids some dinner, and I would like this to be all wrapped up before then."

Marcus pointed down the hall. "I just have to go into your bedroom. That's the last place before we can finish up here."

John jumped out of his recliner ungracefully, and then tried to recover as if he wasn't incredibly anxious about Marcus going into the bedroom. "The bedroom? How come? I mean, you didn't really…well, I mean—" he floundered over his words, giving him away. That is, if Marcus allowed him to give himself away.

"Like I said before, I am just walking throughout the property trying to hit on heat signatures if you will. Any place in or around the house where I feel the presence more fully. Is it all right if I take one last look in your room? I understand that it is a more private area than other sections of the house. I would just really like to get a full assessment." Marcus grinned and then grimaced, hoping both looked convincing to the man standing in the living room.

John shifted from one foot to the other, making it look like he was postponing using the toilet. "Yeah, okay. Sorry. Go ahead. Just don't take too long, huh?"

Marcus raised his hands in surrender. "I promise. Lickety split."

John's eyes narrowed as he noticed the burst blood vessels in Marcus's eyes. He gestured to his own eyes as he asked, "You doing all right? Your eyes are all red."

Marcus nodded his head and tried on a smile. "Sorry, I found myself getting sick in your backyard. I tried to vomit as far out of the way as possible. My apologies."

Marcus watched as John physically relaxed. "It's okay. I'm sorry you're not feeling well." A moment of hesitation. "Well, if you need anything you know where I am." Marcus nodded.

As he walked down the hall, Marcus let out the breath he had been holding. "That was intense," he said under his breath.

You're telling me. In some strange way Marcus found comfort having someone with him at all times. He was sure he would grow weary of it at some point, probably pretty quickly once Craig joined the sublet. But for now, it was almost pleasant.

Marcus opened the door to the bedroom and closed it behind him softly. "Okay, what do we do in here?"

Isn't it obvious? The question came with an unspoken 'duh' and an eye roll.

"Can I get some spicy mayo with the sarcasm, smarty pants?"

Sorry. I didn't realize I had to walk you through this like it was your first time putting together a piece of furniture. Marcus let it sit in the air, unwilling to be baited into speaking any further. It took a few seconds, but Maria continued. *You need to rip up the carpet where you saw the pentagram in the vision. I honestly can't believe he thought I would never notice he put in new carpet. Bless his heart, he tried to match the color, and I might have believed him if he simply told me he spilled something and thought replacing the carpet was the best option. I need you to stand in the middle of the pentagram once you reveal it. This is where the most energy will emanate from in order for you to enter his zone.*

"His zone? Sort of like your Garden Room?"

Exactly.

Marcus stopped moving. "I don't think I want to know what the room of a sicko like Craig looks like. I can't believe you didn't tell me this was why I was here. I didn't get him killed; he did that by way of his own perverted actions. I wish I could say I was sad that he is dead, but I can't. We are supposed to forgive, but anyone who would do that to a child—" he couldn't finish the sentence. Tears rimmed his eyes.

But now you understand why I want him away from my family. You understand how desperate I am.

Marcus nodded and swiped at his eyes to clear them. He searched his memory for where the pentagram had been in the vision. When he was fairly certain he remembered the spot, he looked around for scissors or a knife and found a pair of scissors sitting near John's laptop. He then went back to the spot he imagined was correct for where the pentagram was located. Maria let out a frustrated sigh. *Seriously? Stop. Take three steps that way. To your left. Look down. You see it? Please tell me you see it.*

Marcus did as he was instructed, and then he saw a mark on the carpet. Once he had spied it, he was surprised he didn't find it before. It was a poor job at best. He was going to say something to Maria to try and break the tension, but he felt her waving it off in his head, *You're not going to need to tear up the carpet, just stand over the pentagram.*

Marcus stood tall and backed into the center of the piece of carpeting. "You think this is good en—" before he could even finish the thought, he felt a strong presence directly in front of him. *Never mind. I think I found him.*

The presence was incredibly strong. It felt just as sinister but completely different from the demon in the shed. He found it hard to concentrate, his thoughts slipping around in his mind as if they had been covered in grease. It was a very disorienting feeling, and it took everything in Marcus to calm his head and focus. The dance began.

"Craig, I know you are here. And I would like to come visit you. Would that be all right?" Marcus felt the air drop in temperature and he more felt than heard the reply.

"What do you want with me? Why do you want to come into my sanctum?" The voice was so loud in his head that Marcus almost covered his ears. The volume mentally, audibly, and psychically was not an accident. Craig was trying to keep him off-balance.

"I want to talk to you. I feel we have much to discuss. Wouldn't you agree?" Marcus tried to keep his tone as neutral as possible, but deep down he was terrified. He truly did not want to see what this person's *sanctum* looked like, but he knew he needed to visit.

"What do I have to discuss with a piece of shit like you? You destroyed me. Took my kid away from me." The air in front of Marcus shimmered with rage. Marcus felt as though his eyes were vibrating in his skull. He closed them to regain his composure.

"I know you are mad at me, but that doesn't mean we should resort to calling names. Why don't we have a face-to-face. Just you and me." Marcus's tone was almost chummy, which made him want to throw up. The last thing he wanted was to be chummy with a child molester. But he had to break through somehow.

"What about that bitch? I haven't felt her around for a while. Where'd she go?" Craig was pushing all the buttons, trying to find one to set Marcus off, but he wouldn't take the bait; couldn't allow himself to take it.

"Your sister-in-law is in the garage, where you cannot harm her. I promise that it will be just the two of us. We can have a chat. And then

I'll leave you be. How does that sound?" Marcus could feel his breath speeding up, and he made a conscious effort to slow it down.

"I think that sounds like bullshit, but you want to see my world? You want to take a gander up its skirt? Be my guest."

Without another word the fingers pressed into Marcus's head and he silently screamed out into the universe. When Maria had entered his mind, the sensations were intense but pleasurable; this felt like an unwanted penetration, a forceful insertion that curled him in on himself in an attempt to protect and find solace. But there was none. He had to endure the sensation until it passed. Bile rose into his throat and he offered a guttural grunt to the empty room. His legs gave out and he knelt on the floor. And then he was ripped painfully from his body and flung into oblivion. He shut his eyes, praying for it to end.

The sounds of the physical realm fizzled out and died, replaced by the tortuous sounds of his new surroundings. He took in the noise of children crying, in pain, and his ire rose in his throat like a righteous flame. His eyes shot open and as they adjusted to the dimness of the room he was in, he soaked in all the details, and as he did a sense of dread washed over him. The man who once was solidified in Marcus's mind as a sick, demented individual.

Naked bulbs swung from the ceiling, water dripping past them and sizzling when the two met. There were Polaroids lining every wall, and although he didn't want to see what they were, he knew there was no way to avoid them. And when he saw he broke. Some primal force within him shattered and he knew if he had gotten the chance to meet with Craig in the physical realm one last time, he would bash his head in and gouge out his eyes. He would cut out his tongue and feed it to him, making him choke on his own sin. He would make sure the pain lasted as long as possible in order to account for all the pain he inflicted on his son. Marcus had never had children (with the exception of the recent revelation of one he had no knowledge of), but he knew what was right and what was wrong, and this was not only wrong, it was a cruel and black sin and the separation of the soul from the body. Every single picture hanging around the room was of a young boy, naked, exposed to the camera.

Then Marcus heard the cackling of the sick man and turned to him. Craig was emaciated and black goo dripped from his mouth, puddling all around him on the ground. His eyes were sunken into his skull and he wore nothing but sagging underwear. He almost didn't look human at all. "Do you like my art gallery?" Craig shivered and took a jolting step toward Marcus.

"You are sick. You are twisted. How could you do this to your own son? This is how you want to remember him?" Marcus was aghast and felt like his stomach had betrayed him and was headed up and out of his mouth. He felt like he needed to lean on something but didn't dare touch a single item in the room.

"The innocence of a child is so sweet on the lips; to the touch." Craig shuddered again, and Marcus thought his bones might break. "The purity makes it divine."

Marcus felt himself shaking with rage. "There is nothing divine about abusing a child, you sick freak! Their innocence is to be protected!"

Craig tilted his head back and offered another hacking cackle. "Oh the sensations you feel. They are so delightful."

Marcus dry heaved and stumbled forward a step. "Shut up!"

Craig took another halting step toward Marcus. "Have you ever run your hand through a young boy's hair? The utter ecstasy—"

Marcus cut him off. "Shut up! I demand that you no longer speak of this. You will hear me and hear me well."

The power in his voice caused Craig to stop. He looked at Marcus, blinking slowly, the black tarry substance still oozing out of his mouth. Marcus had to think clearly, or he would be lost in this place forever. He didn't know how he knew it, but it was as real as the ground beneath his knees back in the physical realm.

"You have no claim to your nephew. You do not have the right or permission to hurt him any longer. He is off limits." Craig opened his mouth to protest, but Marcus kept going. "I do the talking now. You stand there and listen. Your nephew calls you the *Dark Man*, which means your intentions are not in his best interest. So, you will stop. Because he is stronger than you. We are all stronger than you. You have no power here or there," he pointed in a vague direction to indicate the physical realm. He had no idea where he was going with this line of thought, but he felt he was on the right track. And the more he could talk, the less Craig could spew his vileness into the empty void.

"Just because your brother gave you permission to enter the house doesn't mean you get to run it. And it certainly doesn't give you permission to mess with your niece and nephew. And it absolutely doesn't give you permission to harm your sister-in-law. You have no rights, you have no authority, you are just a screwed-up nobody whose mind is poison, standing in his underwear slowly withering away. I dispatched your army. They are gone. So, your power is even less now. If you do not turn tail and run, then I will destroy you. You will no longer be in existence, and good riddance to bad rubbish. So, I am giving you this one and only opportunity to head for the hills and never come back. Because if you don't your world is about to get a whole lot worse."

Marcus felt his legs almost give out. They felt like jelly, and he found that he was utterly terrified of Craig and his little twisted dungeon of a room. But if he let on that he was scared, Craig would reach out and suck the fear out of the air, giving himself the strength he needed to regain his power.

Marcus peered around the room and saw that the pictures were growing dim and fuzzy and he knew he was making an impact. That was when the Craig-like creature broke down and started to cry. "I know, man. I'm screwed up in the head." He ripped a swath of hair off his scalp. "I don't know why. I know it's wrong. I know I messed up. I'm sorry." The black goo built up at the corners of his mouth and strung its way to the ground like so much spittle. "I'm an asshole. I should be burned in the deepest pits of hell. Take me there, won't you? Escort me into the fiery depths."

Marcus realized too late that Craig was mocking him. Craig sprang up from the ground with preternatural speed and shoved Marcus to the ground. He crouched on his chest and began to beat against it with his fists, crying out his fake confession as he did. "I shouldn't have touched the poor little boy. He was defenseless. What kind of a monster would do such a thing? Only the kind that deserves to rot in darkness. Certainly not a decent human being! But the devil made me do it, mommy! The devil tickled my brain and gave me thoughts and ideas!"

The fists came down faster and harder. Marcus found himself unable to draw in a full breath. He was slowly suffocating, and he had no idea how to make it stop. And then Craig stopped pounding and drew his face to within inches of Marcus's and smiled, the tarry goo dripping onto Marcus's cheeks and forehead. Marcus felt his gorge rise in his throat and the revulsion was nearly unbearable. Craig smiled his sickly smile, knowing he was impacting Marcus this way.

"I want you to listen to me, you small little excuse for a man. I don't care who you think you are, or how righteous you believe you are, or how much power you think you have, I will eat your soul. I will consume it and it will become a part of me, and then your soul will be as black as mine and you will enjoy all the little activities that I enjoy. And how will you feel then? Hmmm? How will you feel when you are as dark as me?"

Marcus mustered enough strength to raise his head and spit at Craig. He spoke through gritted teeth. "I will never be anything like you, because you are a psychopath, and you deserve all the pain and suffering this world has to offer."

Craig yelled in a rage and raised his fists, meaning to bring them down on Marcus's face. And as his fists descended Marcus's head exploded and he screamed in agony.

CHAPTER 18

This was it. The end. The jig was up. The dance was over. That fat lady had sung her last aria. He had been done in by an angry spirit, a child molester passed on from the earth, with angry fists. The *Dark Man* had gotten the final word and taken him to the afterlife. He felt nothing, saw nothing, heard nothing, a vacuum in the space between the physical and the spiritual, between Earth and the Otherworld. Then he heard a voice that he couldn't quite place: *Keep your eyes closed and listen.*

He knew the voice, but it stayed at the fringes of his memory. Then the dull ache in the back of his skull came into focus and he let out a low, soft groan. *Will you shut up. Listen.* The voice again, not so much angry as urgent. A voice he knew, knew quite well at this point. A woman. Someone. His sister? No, that wasn't right. His sister's name was Maria. Who did he know—it all came to him with the sudden speed of a pellet released from a slingshot; Maria, the mother of Cynthia and Charlie, the wife to John, dead now, but left behind to protect and keep. Sister-in-law to the awful Craig. His mind reeled. He felt himself pitch sideways, creating an overwhelming sense of vertigo, and he thought he might keep tipping until he arrived underneath this world, and then he would be stuck.

Open your ears. This is important. The voice was now filled with anger as well as urgency. Marcus tried to focus, and his ears slowly cleared along with his head. He tentatively tried to move, but his arms and legs wouldn't cooperate. He was stuck (in between?) somewhere without the use of his arms or legs. His ears cleared enough for him to finally hear the voices.

"What did you want me to do? I found the tea in the crawl space. He didn't drink it." The voice sounded slightly panicked.

Now another voice that almost sounded like that of an airline pilot coming through the loudspeaker to the cabin of the aircraft. *Always with that ...cking poiso...you little...ead.* The voice cut in and out, but the intent was there. *John and Craig,* Marcus thought.

Yes. You need to listen to them, but don't open your eyes. They think you are out cold. The voice startled Marcus and he hoped his body hadn't actually flinched, but he was afraid that was a bet he would have lost. He held his breath for a few seconds, waiting for the inevitable footsteps that would come return him to his slumber; instead, the voices continued.

"I had some left over, and I figured it would—" he was cut off abruptly by the voice in the monitor: *You figured. I can't believe we came from the same mother. You can be so fu...nse somet...know that?*

When John responded he sounded like a small child who was trying to find a way to be heard. "I'm sorry, Craigy, I thought I did it right. I thought I had his trust." Marcus realized John had reverted to the younger brother, calling his brother 'Craigy', which he was sure Craig didn't approve of, especially in this moment. He could even see John in his mind's eye with his head down, toeing the ground in contrition, attempting to dig himself a hole he could hide in until the tongue lashing was finished.

All you ever do is think. Nev...ollow through. Craig sounded absolutely livid, but maybe that was partly the static that kept interrupting his words, making it sound like he was maxing out the speaker in the portable device.

There was a long moment of silence, and Marcus could've sworn he heard John sniffling. Marcus wondered what could have happened to cause such an unhealthy dynamic between them. He didn't have to wait long for his answer.

When Craig spoke again it was in a soft tone, one Marcus recognized as an attempt to regain his lost audience's trust. The words came through this time with crystal clarity, and by the end, Marcus wished there had been some static to filter out the words.

I know how difficult it used to be. I know because we were in it together. When Uncle Simon would come in from out of town. You remember Simon Says *as well as I do. What he said we did, or we suffered the consequence. And you only got a little bit of that. I made sure he focused his attention on me. I was the big brother; still am. So, when Uncle Simon would come stay the night, I would excitedly call out that I wanted him to stay in my room. I had to protect you. It is the big brother's job to protect his little brother. And I did the best I could. But that kind of shit will mess with your head, Johnny. That kind of shit will poison your head and make you start to believe things, to wonder about things, to want to pass things along in order to alleviate the pain, the agony of what was happening.*

Marcus heard John take a step toward the monitor. "I have never touched a kid! Never! I have never done that!" He screamed at his brother, and Marcus wondered where the children were. As he listened, he could hear the television from the other room; John had turned up the volume so they wouldn't hear their father communing with their dead uncle.

Because I took that burden on. I took it on for the both of us. You never told that wife of yours about what happened to us did you? Silence, but the turmoil inside Marcus was very loud; Maria was furious at the audacity of her brother-in-law, while simultaneously incredibly sad for her husband. *I didn't think so. She had no clue; no idea the torture we endured. I told Janet and she was afraid for our child. She tried to get him out of there, tried to take my son away from me. That whore thought she had a right to my son, while every night I saw the glaze in her eyes, every morning I dealt with her hangovers.*

The silence this time was absolute; the house did not creak, no one breathed, the monitor fell silent, it was as if time itself had come to a complete standstill. Marcus was afraid they were going to notice he was awake and end their conversation. He gambled on thinking to Maria, not knowing if Craig was able to catch any of the telepathy: *Is this stuff you found out after you were dead?*

Maria didn't respond for about a minute, and when she did her voice was clogged, as if she had been crying and was trying to pretend everything was okay. *I had a thought. But I didn't know the extent until after I passed. Otherworld knowledge can be an unwanted massive head rush, like I've said.*

I am so sorry. The words felt paltry and weak in the face of what he had just heard, but it was all he could muster.

Maria spoke again, quietly and calmly; she had regained her composure. *There's more.* Marcus felt himself shudder and bit his lip to keep from moving further.

"I didn't know he did more to you." John sounded like a whipped dog. Craig owned him now, and he was about to sign the deed to John's soul.

And I know you have some nostalgia associated with poison. I understand that. But back then that is all we had. We weren't big enough or strong enough to defend ourselves, so we had to use what was available to us. The car crash was fortuitous. I listened to the police talk to our parents about it, and they said that he had smashed so hard into the telephone pole they recommended a closed casket funeral. They even asked if there was any interest in doing a toxicology report to see if he had anything in his system that could have caused the accident. Mom and dad said that he didn't even drink, and that it was probably the new rain that had just started. So, we got away with that one, little brother. No more questions, no ifs ands or buts. And we were free of him.

"It doesn't sound to me like you have ever been free of him. It sounds like he got in and stayed." John sounded tired, as if listening to the twisted tale of his youth had aged him twenty years, which mentally and spiritually it may have done just that. Marcus heard John thump down onto the ground.

Some things never leave you. And I can't be blamed for that. I did what I had to, and you're right, he stayed with me. It was the price I had to pay.

"So, what do we do? How do *you* think I should kill him?" The matter-of-fact quality of the question made the hairs on the back of Marcus's neck stand on end. He knew by the tone of John's voice that he was ready to do what he had to in order to finish the task. It was time to think fast or this time he would truly be joining the other side of the divide.

Marcus ran ideas through his head and discarded most of them. He settled on opening his eyes very briefly to figure out where he was in the house; in John's bedroom was his assumption, but he wanted to be sure. His eyes opened and he glanced around and took in as much as he could before he could be discovered: he was sitting in a chair essentially where he had been standing when John had supposedly bludgeoned him to incapacitate him, John was sitting on the floor leaning against his bed with the monitor in his hand, his free hand covering his eyes, the door to the bedroom was closed. Marcus didn't dare risk more time looking around and closed his eyes again.

He was running out of time rapidly, but a plan was not coming to him. What came out of the monitor next dashed all thoughts from his head in an instant: *Grab the butcher knife from the kitchen and jam it through the back of his neck. That should sever his spinal cord and make him choke to death on his own blood.*

Marcus went completely cold and began to panic. Luckily, he remained physically still, but the alarm inside was at a fever pitch and he didn't know if he would even be able to remember what he had for breakfast in this state. He felt a cooling hand settle over his mind, which calmed him a bit, made him focus on the odd sensation that was now in his head. When Maria spoke, she was perfectly calm, no sense of urgency in her voice. *Let's think about this. You have two, maybe three minutes at the least; eight to ten minutes if John thinks of clean up and puts a tarp or plastic down on the ground. You've seen the shed, he is a bit of a neat freak, so my money is on the latter.*

Uh-huh was all Marcus could muster. The hand was calming, but he was still terrified. He couldn't imagine it ending with a knife to the back of the neck. Would it hurt or would he be instantly transported to the *other side?* He guessed that depended on how quickly the knife went through him. The thought sent another shudder through him, which he was fairly certain John would have seen if he had removed his hand from his eyes. When nothing happened John took a calm, deep breath.

You need to get yourself together, bud. I'm in here too, remember. So, it's not just you at risk.

I thought you said you would be fine after I died…well, fine in the sense that you would carry on in the Otherworld. Your spirit will just return to its regularly scheduled programming; tune in next time at the same Bat-time same Bat-channel. Marcus began to panic again.

Different deaths lead to different outcomes. Maria's voice was still calm and cool, like a light breeze on a hot summer day. But the breeze wasn't quite strong enough to take Marcus down a notch or two. *I don't know what would happen to me if you were to die violently, but I'm fairly certain if you die peacefully of natural causes that you would simply exhale me back out into the universe. Violence complicates everything.*

Yeah, that's cool. Sounds good. Sure. Why not? Marcus felt as if he were losing touch with reality, accepting his fate before it had arrived. He needed to calm down but couldn't find his way there. His mind wandered to his sister who had died in a very unpeaceful way and he began to wonder what became of her soul as she violently departed from the physical realm. His mind took him on a tangent into the universe of what-ifs and could have beens and he was lost.

His father drank himself to death; was that considered natural causes or violent or something else entirely? And he had no real idea what happened to his mother. All of that had been a lie; and how about his other sibling? His family jumbled in his mind creating a Rubik's Cube of confusion. He tried to turn the cube this way and that in an attempt to reach a single conclusion, but he felt himself slipping further from his current situation. In the back of his mind he realized he was coping with the inevitable by separating himself, but he didn't care anymore. Maybe this is what Maria felt when she knew she was being poisoned by her husband. Maybe this was his acceptance, and by flitting about in his past trying to make sense of things he wouldn't feel the knife as it slipped into the back of his neck and poked through the front, making him a human shish kabob.

He felt something tugging at his mind and tried to shoo it away. It was better in the confusion; it was easier. But the pulling continued, and it took him a moment to realize the feeling wasn't in his head but was something that was physically occurring. Reluctantly, he returned to the present and felt John tugging on his bindings to make sure he wouldn't escape while he went and got the instrument of death that would end his life and begin the next. And that made him think about John's children and if their uncle would tell them about what happened to the man that had been in their house, and how traumatized they might be with that information lurking in their subconscious. Finally, that brought him to his own child, whom he had only discovered that day existed somewhere out in the world. A child that he had never met and would never have a chance to meet when all was said and done. So, now he would leave with a regret he didn't know he would have. But another thought occurred to him in almost the same moment: He was calm now. His mind had calmed to the point where he was able to think again. He had come full circle back to clarity, and maybe he could figure a way out of this; maybe this wasn't the final countdown, the end of the tunnel, the ultimate demise.

Marcus heard John in his ear say to the nearly empty room, "I'll be right back, Craig." And when the door to the bedroom opened and shut, it sobered Marcus up in an instant; it brought him fully back.

Welcome back. Marcus sensed a little smile in Maria's voice when she spoke. *Are you ready to save us now?*

Yes. But I don't know how.

Think about where you are right now.

Bedroom.

Where though?

In the same spot I was in when I went to Craig's room in the Otherworld.

So, that would mean... Marcus could see her hand twirling in his head, begging for him to make the connection. It took him a few seconds, but when he finally figured it out, the dominoes fell into place and he was ready to knock them down.

I am sitting on the Pentagram. I can get back to Craig. If I can get him to join us, maybe…but John will be back soon.

Time moves different in the Otherworld. I'm not going to say you have a ton of time to work with, but you should have enough if you work quickly.

Any ideas on how to get him to join this unholy matrimony once I get back there?

Ask real nice like? The cheery tone to Maria's voice underlined the phrase, and Marcus smiled despite the situation he found himself in. He took a deep breath, hoping that Craig wouldn't notice the shift in body language and tattle to John before he could complete the task.

Marcus concentrated, allowing himself to be led by Maria toward Craig's room. He tried not to focus on the fact that if he failed the *Dark Man* would get his way and be able to wreak havoc on his niece and nephew for as long as he wanted. His focus was on saving them, giving them a safe haven to be able to attempt to live a normal life. With these thoughts coursing through his mind he felt that Maria's hope was the same and their emotions intermingled into a single resolve. He felt himself begin to slip, and as he disappeared, he heard the door to the bedroom open and John say, "I need to put some plastic down, or this is going to be a big ol' mess to clean up later."

Marcus's final thought as he went through the veil was, *Oh thank God.*

CHAPTER 19

Marcus assumed that after all the 'sliding' he had done over the course of the day that he would be used to it, but it still felt like being transferred from one body to another piece by piece. It was like the most extreme out of body experience one could have, and it still took him a few moments to orient himself once he was in the dark, dungeon-like room of Craig, the *Dark Man*. The musty smell returned instantly, and the Polaroids still papered the walls. Marcus made every effort to avoid looking at them; he needed to have an absolute focus, and the pictures infuriated him to the point of making sloppy mistakes, and he didn't have the time for any slip ups.

At first, he couldn't locate Craig, and he started to panic again. Maybe he wasn't here after all and was indeed telling John that he needed to hurry up and finish the deed before his prize could escape. But then he heard a rhythmic sound, a sound that resembled someone squeezing fish, and he furrowed his brow, trying to place the sound. A voice rose up in the darkness. "I'm in control. I'm in control. This is my control." The squishy sound continued and when the realization finally came to Marcus, he frowned and looked disgusted; Craig was getting off on his own power, he was almost certain of it. Marcus rounded a small corner and sure enough, Craig was sitting in a corner, by the grace of God turned away from him, stark naked, his right arm moving almost violently. He cleared his head, trying not to think about what he was witnessing; Craig thought he was alone. He was so focused on the job at hand that he hadn't sensed Marcus entering his personal space. Marcus and Maria had the advantage of surprise. Craig's voice filled the room again. "I am in control. I control this space. This is my control."

Marcus composed his thoughts and tried to figure out what he was going to say and how he was going to accomplish his task. After a few seconds of unsuccessful brainstorming he decided he was going to have wing it; he didn't really have any other choice; the clock in his head was ticking down rapidly.

"Why don't you put yourself away and look at me." Marcus spoke with authority, hoping to stagger Craig into a disoriented state of mind. It partially worked because Craig started to turn and fell off the chair onto the ground. Marcus looked over Craig's head. "Put yourself away so we can talk."

Craig smiled his oozy sinister smile and stood up facing Marcus, unashamed. "Do I make you nervous? Can't you even look at me? Are you ashamed because you have dirty thoughts too?"

But Marcus didn't take the bait. He looked Craig directly in the eyes and said, "Not at all. If you stand there in front of me in this way you dishonor and shame your parents and brother. You are a coward." Marcus held his gaze and waited. It took a few seconds, but Craig finally shifted his eyes to the side and in the next instant he was fully clothed, although the clothes looked about as raggedy and dirty as he did.

Oh, thank you Jesus. That thing is ugly as sin.

To be fair, none of them are about to win a beauty pageant. Out loud Marcus said, "I'm sorry you suffered at the hands of your uncle when you were a kid."

Craig rolled his eyes, which made an unnerving squeaking sound when he did. "You going to psychobabble me into standing down, going away, disappearing? You don't think I've heard all the arguments about how I can get help because what was done to me was terrible and I can change my mindset? Quack, quack. Get out of here, doc."

"I don't care what you think about it all. I simply want to acknowledge that you were done wrong and that isn't okay. But it also doesn't give you the right to perpetuate the same thing on someone else." Marcus was stalling for time (no time), trying to come up with a good enough argument to gain the upper ground. He figured Craig had heard all the stories and examples and reasons for why he was the way he was, besides the fact that he was a bit past help from a psychoanalyst at this point. "I also know that when you are in those situations you feel powerless, so you need to regain your power, which means you need to make someone else feel powerless. It's not about the sexuality of it all, it's about the need to be the strongest."

"Gee, thanks Freud." Craig made a crude gesture with his hand.

Where are you going with all this? Maria asked, a little impatiently. She knew full well the clock was ticking and wasn't ready to find out what happened when there was a violent expulsion of life she was connected to so viscerally.

Not a clue. I'm just trying to come up with the right thing to say and not run out of time in the process. If you have any ideas, I am open to them. Maria didn't respond, which to Marcus was as good as her telling him to keep on. He took a deep breath, trying to think through his next plan of attack. "I was thinking about the elasticity of a child's mental capabilities, but one thing that tends to stretch that rubber band out and wear it down is repetition. I imagine you felt pretty worn down by the time your uncle was done with you. Do you really want to do the same to your nephew? Do you really want to wear him down until he reaches *his* point of no return and passes on this sickness to another generation? How selfish can you be?"

Marcus thought that maybe raising Craig's ire would have an unsteadying effect on him that would allow an opportunity to coerce him into a conversation within Marcus's mind. He hoped that would be the case. But the look on Craig's face told Marcus he was not about to be tempted that easily. "Oh, poor little Charlie. He has to deal with a little bit of pain and suffering. Boohoo. At least he'll learn about it before the world forces it on him."

"So, ruin him from the Otherworld? Force him from the spirit realm? That sounds like a mercy, doesn't it?" Marcus's words dripped with sarcasm, but Craig either didn't notice or chose not to, and smiled and nodded his head in agreement. "Why not give his dad a chance to walk him through it all when he deems it is the right time? Why do you think you are *so* important that you are the only one that can give him the message?"

Craig scratched his head, but to Marcus it sounded more like his scalp was ripping off his skullcap. The sound was sickening, and it turned Marcus's stomach. "That little pissant? He is the weakest little mama's boy I've ever seen. To be honest, I'm surprised he even knew how to use his tallywacker to inseminate his stupid wife." Venom dripped off every word Craig spoke.

"Do you think all women are stupid? I mean, I get it. In my opinion they're only good for satisfying and cooking dinner." Maybe here was an inlet to catching Craig off his guard. Marcus could only hope that

Craig thought he was sincere, and he tried to push the thought to Maria that he was simply trying to get a rise out him. *I'm sorry. I'm sorry. I'm sorry.*

Craig let a dry cackle escape his mouth. "They don't give any pleasure. They are good for one thing and one thing only: Carrying on the genetic line. If I could create my own offspring, I wouldn't need a woman ever again."

"Don't you think that maybe that's because you were taught at a young age that sex isn't pleasure? That sex is pain and terror and helplessness? Maybe that's your problem with women." Marcus's hopes disappeared as he watched Craig's face closely, and Craig looked like he was bored of the conversation.

You're losing him talking in circles like this. We need a solution, and soon. Maria was starting to sound impatient and a little scared. Marcus could handle the first emotion, but the last one filled him with a creeping dread.

It's like he wants to bite, but then backs out. He's smarter than I thought. Marcus was frustrated, his plans falling flat, his attempts being rerouted back to him. How could he end this if his target didn't seem to care about anything? He seemed to have a nihilistic attitude about everything, which lent to a more sociopathic tendency. The only piece that seemed to interest him, that had given a rise at all, was the topic of women. And just like that it hit Marcus like a slap across the face. He knew the Achilles heel. And he knew how to strike. He was about to get his way and save Maria's children in the process.

Craig seemed to notice the change in the way Marcus was carrying himself, a glint in his eye that wasn't there before. He tried a smile, but Marcus could tell it was as fake as a three-dollar bill. He was nervous for the first time since their interaction had begun. Marcus felt the knife hovering around the edge of his physical body, but he knew he needed to let this feeling linger for Craig for a bit longer; make him more susceptible to what was to come. If Marcus could get Craig to speak first Marcus would know he had a chance. He returned the smile to Craig, waiting anxiously. Craig shifted from one foot to the other and licked his lips, his eyes flicking back and forth rapidly. It was taking too long. He was too smart; he wouldn't take the bait. All of this was for nothing. Marcus was about to die, Maria would be sent off who knew where, and Craig would control his own universe and ruin his nephew's life. But he didn't let any of that show on his face. A few more seconds, that's all. Just a few more seconds.

And then Craig broke the tension. "What are you smiling at, you asshole!" Marcus had him, and his grin segued nicely into a genuine smile.

"Your mother knew." Marcus didn't elaborate. He didn't have to; the color immediately drained from Craig's face. And then the whole room shimmered and went fuzzy at the edges. Marcus swallowed to keep his breakfast from rising. He had hit it. Now he just needed the final nail; the nail that would drive the entire story home. "And she did nothing about it." The room went out of focus again, and this time it took longer to come back, and when it did Craig was a few steps closer to Marcus. But Marcus held his ground. Craig was shaking, his hands almost vibrating. He looked like a sped up moving picture. He was losing his grasp on his own sacred space if you could call a den this sick and twisted *sacred*. Marcus concluded that was the exact wrong word but was right to Craig. "She did nothing, because Simon was her brother."

Craig started to foam at the mouth, the oily goo bubbling out and falling to the ground. "And she knew that you killed your uncle. And she did nothing. Because you were her son." Now Craig's jaw was working up and down, and he looked like a mechanical character at a kids' party restaurant. He was almost there. One more turn of the screw and Marcus would have him right where he wanted him. It was time to finish this. "And your brother knows nothing about this. He thinks you are the only two that know anything about what happened to you and what you did about it." And with those words out, Marcus took a step back and waited for the lunge; waited for the shriek of rage and the bum rush.

But neither of those things happened. Instead, Craig blinked a couple times and his head appeared to clear. *Come on!* Marcus and Maria chimed in together. Craig cocked his head to one side and scratched his head again; that sound of forever being scalped. "You heard the conversation. How else would you know about all this? You were faking it the whole time. You were awake. You dirty, rotten son of a bitch. You sneaky little bastard!"

In a single instant Marcus knew it was lost. He had to think and think fast, or Craig would be gone, and this would be over, and not in the favor of the side of good. The room began to waver, Craig slipped in and out of existence, the Polaroids on the wall flew off the walls in a whirlwind around Marcus, likely in an attempt to distract him while Craig made his escape. He was losing him, and he was well aware of the consequences if he did. His mind went into overtime. He had to come up with some good reason to make him stay, and then the voice in his head gave him his answer, simply by speaking the words: *It's over. If he leaves, we are done for.*

As Marcus watched Craig fade out one last time, he yelled one word, the name of the voice in his head: "Maria!" There was a moment where Marcus thought he was too late. He repeated the phrase over and over in his head hoping someone would hear his plea: *Please, please, please, please.*

When Craig returned it sucked all the air out of the room and Marcus felt as if his lungs would explode. His nose started to bleed but he didn't raise his hand to check and see if that was real. Craig was enraged. The fury in his eyes was unmatched by anything Marcus had borne witness to up to that point. Marcus could feel the heat of Craig's hatred like a sunburn on his face. And when he spoke it sounded like a thousand voices joining in a dissonant choir, demanding an answer from Marcus. "WHERE IS SHE?!"

Marcus watched Craig seethe, looking like a wild animal whose baby had been killed in front of it. He had him back and there was no way he was going to lose him again; Marcus could see that in Craig's eyes. He had found the lynchpin and pulled it out from under Craig's sanity. Now, all that remained was to bring him into the fold. And he thought he knew exactly how to do it. He simply had to hope there was still time.

Craig took a step toward Marcus, his fists clenched, waiting for an answer. Marcus took a step toward Craig and pointed at his own temple. "She's in here. She's with me." Craig let out an enraged cry, which shook the entire room, vibrating it until Marcus thought it would crack open like an egg that has been smashed onto the ground.

"I want to talk to her. I want to talk to her now." Another step toward Marcus.

"If you want to talk to her you have to come inside. You have to join us. Then you can talk to her all you want." Marcus took another step toward Craig. They were almost nose to nose and Marcus could smell the decay wafting off Craig in sheets of malodorous heatwaves.

"I will speak to her here and now." He looked into Marcus's eyes, and then through his eyes, searching desperately for Maria. "Come out, come out wherever you are. Come get your medicine. You think you can turn my brother against me? You think you can break our bond? How dare you!"

Marcus reached out and grabbed the sides of Craig's head and pulled him close. He felt greasy and not all there, almost as if he were simply wearing a skin suit that he had found lying around. The skin didn't fit over the skeleton quite right and it was disconcerting, but Marcus held on for dear life. And then he spoke, but not in his voice. Maria spoke through his mouth directly to Craig. "Come on in, you piece of shit!"

With a yell of pure rage Craig began to disintegrate in Marcus's hands. Marcus felt it as Craig's skin gave way to muscle and then bone and then nothing. Marcus's hands clapped together forcefully as Craig's semblance of a corporeal body dissipated into thin air. And then Marcus felt Craig's essence climb inside his brain and take hold. But Craig's anger distracted him, and before he had a chance to take over his new host, Maria and Marcus turned on him, constructing a prison of the mind just for Craig. A place where he would exist but wouldn't be able to escape from no matter how hard he tried. At least that was the hope. Maria and Marcus didn't know if it would hold him forever, but all they needed for now was this moment of capture.

The cell they conjured for their new guest was clear; there was no way either of them wanted to have any blind spots when it came to the monster in their midst. Craig continued to scream and began banging his head against the invisible walls, leaving grease marks and bits of hair and scalp behind. In mere moments the walls cleared, allowing perfect vision inside so he had nowhere to hide.

Maria stepped up to the cell and looked in at Craig. It took him almost a full minute to realize she was there, but when he did, he focused all his filth onto her. "You filthy little bitch! Who do you think you are? You meddling wh—" and with a wave of her hand she cut off the sound. Marcus could see that he was still screaming and banging his head against the walls, but it had gone eerily silent.

Marcus felt a band of vertigo slide across his vision as he recognized that he was inside his own head. He imagined this was only possible because they were in the Otherworld, but it was an entirely new and odd sensation that he neither liked nor disliked. Maria's eyes were red-rimmed, and her face was puffy from crying. And Marcus realized that he too was crying. The adrenaline was wearing off and the reality of the situation was hitting home. They had done it. They had captured Craig. It was over.

But it really wasn't over. Not yet. They needed to make sure John didn't skewer Marcus in the physical world. Marcus knew there was a little maintenance to be done first. Maria looked at him and he took a step back, glad to be able to take a quick break from the mental gymnastics he had been performing.

Maria paced in front of Craig's cell as she ran down the information for him. "Hey Craig. First of all, I need you to understand that I always knew you were a piece of garbage. Why do you think I kept you away from my family as much as possible?" The way she was speaking it seemed to Marcus like she was beginning a TED Talk. Craig made crude gestures from behind the wall and his mouth kept flapping, so Maria made the entire wall go opaque with the exception of his face. Anywhere Craig moved the clear box followed, but the majority of his body was a blur. "And now you exist here with us. Marcus and I will be your constant companions from here on. Neither of us cares about what you think of us," she paused to tap on the wall to emphasize her point, "so you might as well shut up and listen to what I have to say.

Because it is very important. I assure you."

Marcus was curious about how much control he had over his own mind, never having been in the position before to find out. He thought about a chair and one appeared in front of him, but then he decided on a recliner and the chair was replaced by an old leather recliner. He sat down to wait out the rest of the one-sided conversation, ever aware of the slim time frame they were working with currently.

Maria watched Craig until he calmed down and simply followed her with his hate-filled eyes. "Good," she began. "Now that we have some semblance of calm, I will explain what is going to happen next. Your brother is going to poke a knife through our lovely host's neck in the next few minutes, giving him another spot from which to whistle. Here's the problem with that scenario. I've done some research, and I have it on good authority that if we are stuck in Marcus's head when he expires, if the death is a violent one, we will be shot into oblivion. That means no more you and no more me. We will be extinguished.

"That doesn't bode well for either of us. What we need is Mr. Marcus here to die of natural causes sometime down the road. Does that make sense?" She didn't wait for a reply. Tick-tock goes the clock. "So, what I need from you, sicko of the century, is for you to speak up when we go back to the physical world. And this is the part that really matters…" Marcus listened as Maria explained the plan, and Craig sat and listened from his cell built for one. He even nodded once or twice to show his understanding. It didn't take long for Maria to finish up, and when she did, she turned to Marcus. "We ready to go back?"

Marcus nodded his head, wondering if he sent a thought to Maria if Craig would hear it as well. He figured it was worth the risk. *Will he do his part?*

Maria smiled, which eased Marcus's mind. *He will if he knows what's good for him. We can't keep him locked up forever, I can already feel him trying to find his escape hatch. We just need to make sure that we are safely locked away before he makes his triumphant return.* And, as if to accentuate her remark, Craig banged his head against the wall again and the faintest crack appeared. It was gone in the next moment, but it had been there.

And then it was time to slide one last time.

CHAPTER 20

Marcus closed his eyes when the slip began, taking in the experience through the motion itself, rather than the sensation of watching the world tilt like sand in an hourglass. He found the experience to be quite alluring and wished faintly that he had done it this way every other time. And when he felt the motion come to a stop, he slowly opened his eyes to find blood dripping down onto his pant leg. His first thought was that he was too late, or, more accurately, just in time to see himself die. But when he took a deep breath in and his lungs expanded and there wasn't a gurgle of blood in his throat, he lifted his head quickly and turned it to see John standing behind him with gloves on and the butcher knife in his hand. It was raised, ready to strike, but he froze in midair at the sudden reappearance of his victim's consciousness.

They locked eyes and Marcus could see the determination in John's eyes falter, and for a brief second, Marcus thought maybe his resolve would dissipate and they wouldn't need to call on Craig. Then the light shifted in John's eyes and Marcus opened his mouth and yelled, "NOW!"

There was the briefest of hesitation from John, who was most likely confused that the man before him that he was about to stab had encouraged him to finish the deed, or at least *seemed* to be encouraging the act. In that moment Marcus felt Craig fill his head and he was very abruptly privy to Craig's life; from the abuse he took as a child to the abuse he gave as an adult. He saw the hours Craig had spent weeping and self-flagellating in an attempt to rid himself of his own demons that were brought to him by his uncle. There were relationships that faltered quickly, leaving Craig to blame himself for the way it all went, and telling himself he would get the help he needed to be able to step out of his prison. And he saw the repetition of the process as he tried and failed and got angry and was vengeful and seized opportunities to gain power and control over others. Marcus felt Craig's heart slowly harden and grow cold until he knew that Craig had simply accepted his fate. He came to the realization in his own mind that he could not escape or outrun the atrocities his uncle had visited upon him, so he decided to embrace it and to hell with everyone else.

And then Marcus's heart stopped when he saw Craig's memory of holding his own son. The conversations he had in the mirror every night about how he would never harm a hair on the boy's head, no matter what the demons told him to do. He watched his interactions with his strung-out wife and the lack of control and power he had within the relationship; nothing he did mattered or had an impact. She did what she wanted when she wanted and the only thing that kept Craig from beating her was the ultimate knowledge that she would then be able to take his boy away from him.

Marcus saw the first time he hurt the boy. He grabbed his wrist too hard and felt a tiny pop, dislocating it with little effort. The boy cried and cried and wouldn't stop and Craig didn't know what to do, because his wife was out again, dead to her family, living her own private hell.

So, Marcus shook the boy enough to make him stop crying and, in the process, popped the wrist back into its socket. And Marcus watched Craig at the mirror again, hating himself for what he had done, and vowing that if he ever hurt his son again, he would just kill himself. He could never inflict pain again on his beloved one. End it and call it a night.

When the real abuse started, Marcus tried to close his eyes and turn away, but he had to see, was made to see the cruelty and hatred that had filled Craig again. He detached himself from the acts he committed, and the first few times he gave himself his speech in the mirror. Then the speeches stopped, and the abuse continued. It acted as an aphrodisiac to Craig, and he started to revel in the feeling. Even if the rest of the world came down on him, at least he had dominion over his son. And by the end, when his fellow inmates stabbed him to death in his jail cell, he sat and cackled at them while they did it. He was dead before he died.

Then it was over. And Marcus felt compassion for this man, not within the pain he inflicted on others, including his son, but for what the world had given to him and how he fought in order to break the cycle. He hadn't fought hard enough, didn't seek the help he needed, and chose his path in the end, but there was a human side to him intermixed with all the awful acts he committed. Marcus didn't want to feel compassion, not even a hint of pity, especially after having to bear witness to the atrocities of his life, yet it sat there within him like a peach pit that would never grow into a tree; a dead compassion that simply existed. Another unwanted gift from a simple house call he had made; the last house call he would ever make.

All of this happened within the split second that it took for John to strengthen his resolve and raise the knife to strike. Then Craig called out from within Marcus's body, "No, Johnny, no! You can't do this." And John stopped, a confused look entering his eyes. "Listen to my voice. You know who I am. Don't run me through like a stuck pig."

The knife clattered to the ground, which startled Marcus. He was fascinated by what was happening in this moment. He felt fully aware, and he had full cognitive function over his body, but he had lent his vocal cords to this other person, this other entity within himself. It was a very surreal feeling, and a wave of euphoria passed through Marcus, making him shiver. He could feel the anger still residing in ever sinew of Craig's being, and he could also feel the calm counter force of Maria trying to maintain this delicate balance without giving Craig enough control to take over completely.

John moved in front of Marcus and looked into his eyes, studying them carefully. "Craig?" he asked tentatively, desperately not wanting to have gone totally bonkers in the last ten seconds.

"Yeah, it's me Pinprick." Marcus searched the memory bank and found many instances of Craig calling John by that nickname. Undoubtedly it was a nickname kept strictly between them and was his way of proving it was really him. John's face went ashen and he sat down heavily on the bed, bouncing slightly from the springs.

"What the hell is going on?" John breathed out.

Marcus could see the wheels turning in his head, but it looked as if he was missing a cog or two to complete the revolution of understanding. His mouth worked up and down, trying to find a question or answer that was just outside of his reach.

"Listen up, I know it's hard to know what is happening right now, but Marcus here will explain everything to you." Every word out of Craig's mouth sounded exasperated and pissed. "It's a whole thing. I need you to do something for me, and then I have to go away again.

These assholes won't let me enjoy the party."

John looked absolutely flummoxed, and all he could manage to do was nod his head. Marcus felt bad for the guy; first he conjures his dead brother and invites him into his house, then he kills his cancer riddled wife with poison, then he is convinced that he needs to bring a spirit communicator into his home and kill him, and now he was interacting with his dead brother within the body of another person. Not to mention that he still had yet to discover that his dead wife was also within this other person. That's a rough day, thank you kindly.

"I need you to untie Marcus here and let him explain everything. He says they are on a timeline, so everything has to be done in short order. Listen closely, act quickly, and execute the plan. I'm telling you something, these two are a couple of fu—" and then his voice was cut off, leaving Marcus as the front runner to the operation. Marcus felt Craig get locked away by Maria but could tell that Maria's energy was waning. She was getting tired. They may have stopped the knife from gutting Marcus, but time was still of the essence.

John was still sitting on the bed, trying to sort the whole mess in his brain. He had a dull look on his face, a faraway expression that Marcus didn't like. This next part was of utmost importance, and Marcus felt that if it didn't go smoothly, he might lose his nerve and run out of the house to deal with the voices in his head on his own.

Marcus lowered his head to try and catch John's eyes. "John, I need you to look at me. I need you to focus. Can you hear me?" John continued to stare a hole in the floor, and a little drool escaped his lower lip and fell to the ground in a gooey string. It would do them no good if they had broken him. Then it was all for nothing indeed. Marcus cleared his throat loudly and John's head snapped up and John finally looked at him.

"I can hear you. I'm sorry, I'm just a little lost. I don't understand what is happening." A wave of pity cycled through Marcus's body again. But there would be plenty of time for that later.

"I need you to listen to me and do everything I say. I will explain as much as I am able in the limited time we have." Marcus gestured to the ties and John stood up and grabbed the butcher knife. An irrational thought that John was simply going to end it there no matter what had just occurred, flashed through Marcus's head, but when John sliced through the first rope, Marcus exhaled loudly and brought his hands around front, rubbing his wrists.

Once the ties were severed Marcus gestured for John to sit on the bed and listen closely. He kept reiterating the point, but he felt like John still wasn't fully functional yet.

"A lot has happened in your house today. But, first things first. I need you to call the police. You will tell them that there is a man in your house that is threatening your life." John opened his mouth to protest, but Marcus held a hand up to silence him. "This man is threatening you and your children with a butcher knife. When you make the call, you need to whisper so they think that you are hiding from this man. When they arrive, we will all be in the living room waiting, which means the rest of this has to move very quickly. Grab your cell phone and make the call."

John hesitated for only a moment, and then he moved off to the other side of the bedroom to call the police. There was a sudden banging that made Marcus jump, and he looked toward the door, knowing there was no way anyone could have gotten there so quickly. But the sound didn't come from the door; it came from inside Marcus's head. He turned inward. *Everything okay in there, Maria?*

I'm getting tired. We need to hurry this up if possible. I'm losing control over his cell. There are spiderwebs all over the walls and they are not reforming as quickly.

"Well, that's not good," Marcus said out loud as John turned around, ending the phone call with the police.

"What's wrong?" It appeared that John was ready to accept what was happening. That, or he figured he had cracked for good and was simply going with the flow.

"We need to really hurry this part up. Your family is still not completely out of danger." Marcus heard something shatter in his head and heard the angry voice of Craig say, *Let me talk to my brother you asshole. I demand it.* And then his voice was muffled. And then it was gone. Marcus turned to John and smiled gravely. "You hung up on the police. Won't they be suspicious?"

John's cheeks flushed red. "I told them that I heard you...the man...in my house...coming, so I didn't want to announce where me and the kids were. They said there was a patrol car about ten minutes out and wished I wouldn't hang up the phone. I faked panic and hung up." Marcus now had a little confidence that this might all work out in the end.

"Well, it seems that we have ten minutes for me to unpack a whole tractor trailer full of information." Marcus cleared his throat and began.

"When I arrived at your house today, I had no idea what I was stepping into, and I guess at this point I don't really get to step out of it. I told you that I sensed multiple entities and I was right about that. The conversation with your daughter led to the unlocking of all the answers and the whole story of why I am here." John looked uncomfortable at the mention of that, but Marcus ignored it and continued.

"While I was talking to Cynthia, I ended up having a very in-depth conversation with your wife."

Before he could continue, John placed a hand on his arm. "My brother said these two when he was talking earlier. Is…" his voice nearly gave out, but he took a deep breath and continued. "Is my wife in there with you?"

"She is. And you can speak to her soon. But for now, I really need you to concentrate and shut up." John reluctantly nodded his head.

"Your wife showed me how you summoned your brother into the house and helped me make the connection that he was the one I sent away when I noticed the bruises on his son's body. None of this was a coincidence; it was all very carefully orchestrated by Maria. She has convinced me that in order to protect your family I needed to—" Here Marcus struggled for the right term, and in the blank space he heard another crash, this one louder than the last. And Craig spoke up again: *Can you hear me? John? Can you hear me? Don't listen to their horseshit! Give me a little more time and we can be together ag—* Once again the voice first was muffled and then dissipated completely. Marcus could tell he was gaining a little ground each time. He hoped they would have just enough time for the police to get here before he tried to take control for good. Craig was stronger than Marcus anticipated.

"In order to protect your family, I needed to absorb her and Craig into me and be sent away. The reason I had you call the police was because I have a feeling your brother will gain enough strength to be able to take control without some drastic treatments and a few choice drugs coursing through my system to keep him at bay. If I checked myself into a mental health facility, assuming he hadn't taken over before I could accomplish that, he would most likely be able to escape and your family would be in danger again."

You can count on it.

I'm sorry. I'm trying my hardest, but he is gaining ground.

John took a deep breath. "My brother would never hurt my family. I don't believe it."

Marcus closed his eyes tightly and then looked at John, hoping the blaze in them would capture his full attention. "But he already has. I saw the marks on Charlie. That was your brother."

Tell him it was an accident. It'll never happen again. I swear I'll play nice.

Marcus shook his head to clear it and then continued. "Allowing myself to be incarcerated in a place designed for the criminally insane is the only option we have here. And we need to be ready when the police show up. We have a very slim window for all of this."

John sat up straight and pointed a finger at Marcus. "I want to talk to her."

Marcus nodded. "You will get a chance in a moment. But I need to finish explaining the rest of this." An alarm went off in Marcus's head; a klaxon bell that made him cover his ears from the pain. He felt Craig trying to creep his way into his head and had to focus an enormous amount of energy to hold him back. He understood how keeping him hostage was draining Maria so quickly. His skin crawled and his hair stood on end, but he was able to contain Craig again.

I'm coming for you!

John watched patiently while the man in front of him had a moment to himself, worry written on his face, wondering why he seemed to be in pain. Marcus righted himself and that was when he noticed his nose was bleeding. The spatter on his knee made sense, but he didn't have time to think about anything outside of the information he needed to relay to John.

"First, your wife led me to a stash she had been putting aside for you all before the poison killed her." He reached inside his pockets and pulled out the stacks of bills and handed them to John.

You're giving the money to my family?

Marcus shrugged. *I'm not going to need it.*

He felt Maria begin to cry and blocked it out. Craig tried to intercede again and got only two words out before being shut out. *Gag me.* It seemed Maria's strength had been renewed, at least for the moment. So, Marcus took advantage.

He looked at John who looked back sheepishly. "She knew about the poison?"

"She knew about the poison, but she forgives you. And if you need to pin that on me to help the criminally insane thing stick, that is fine. I don't know how we can prove it, but I'm sure something can be done." Marcus took a breath; he suddenly felt very tired. There was a feeling in his arms, like someone trying to take control of his motor functions. And for a moment, they succeeded. Marcus's right arm reached out toward the money, but at the last second Marcus focused his mind and made Craig recede. He figured he had a minute, maybe two before he lost all control over his own body.

Almost had you that time, you little shit!

Marcus looked at John with a tired smile. "We are running out of time rapidly now. You can talk to your wife, but it has to be brief. Understand?"

John nodded and sat forward on the bed. Marcus receded into his head and took over the guard duties for the time being. It seemed he didn't need to be in the Otherworld to escape into his own head; there was simply a learning curve. He could barely make out the cell Craig was in, and it was covered in spiderwebs where he had banged into it repeatedly, trying to break free. Marcus heard sirens and looked around frantically, hoping it wasn't Craig escaping again. Then he realized the sirens were from the approaching police vehicles.

Marcus was about to take control again when all four walls of Craig's cell shattered, and Craig came straight for him. *Maria! I need your help!*

She appeared a moment later, and together they were able to shackle him to the floor, but they could no longer keep him silent. Marcus knew he would have to ignore him as best as he could in order to finish the final act of this dark, twisted up play. He heard John's desperate voice calling out for his wife and took control once more.

Here I come. And I'm gonna fuck you up but good this time!

"John, you can speak with your wife later. Right now, we need to move to the living room. We need to do it fast. They're almost here." Marcus saw tears streaming down John's face, and in a detached part of his brain Marcus thought that would help sell the story to the cops.

Ready or not, here I come. You're dead, Marcus!

Marcus stood up and grabbed John by the arm. He scooped up the knife as he passed by it and they made their way to the living room. Halfway there, Marcus's legs started to lock up, and they tried to turn on their own (with Craig's help) to escape the plan. The knife in Marcus's hand moved involuntarily toward his chest. With a gigantic last effort, Marcus and Maria clamped him in irons and Marcus regained control of his own legs and arm. Sweat popped out on his forehead and he felt like he could nap for a day or two if someone would simply allow him.

They entered the living room and Maria came forward without any warning. Marcus realized she had complete control, which made him realize that she still had quite a bit of strength left, she was simply saving it for this moment. Luckily, Marcus had learned to trust her, so he didn't fight her on it. They turned to Cynthia and Maria spoke rapidly. "Cynthia, you remember that time you were in that play and

209

you needed to act scared? I need you to do that for mommy right now. I need you to act super scared. Can you do that for me?"

Cynthia stood up and nodded enthusiastically. "Of course. I can do that." Even before the sentence was out of her mouth her face turned to utter terror. Marcus felt bad for a moment, believing the acting himself.

Then they turned to Charlie, and before Marcus knew what was happening, Maria reached out and tweaked his upper arm. He immediately burst into tears and Maria receded, fixing her remaining energy on Craig. There was a bang on the door and Marcus thought, *Showtime. Places everyone.* Then he looked at John, who looked royally angry, probably because this man had just hurt his son. Again, that detached part thought the authenticity of the emotion would help sell the whole thing.

"Police! Open up!" Another banging on the door. And Marcus felt Craig give one last surge and he turned inward to focus on him with Maria. Marcus felt Craig's rage and felt his strength grow in the fury. Another few seconds and it would all be over, one way or another. Everything else happened within the space of one minute.

A police officer kicked in the door and came in with his gun pointed in front of him. Once he saw the scene before him, he holstered his gun and pulled his taser gun from its holder. Three other officers piled in behind him, each following the same action as the first. Marcus now had four tasers pointed directly at him. He looked down lazily and saw the red dots on his chest. From a great distance he heard the lead officer yell for him to drop the weapon. He did not comply. He waited.

As soon as Marcus heard the officer repeat the demand, Maria and Marcus both let go of Craig, and he came forward in a rush of hatred and boiling rage, taking over the shared body wholly. He raised the knife and yelled a tirade of curse words that made the officer's eyes widen. And as he brought the knife in toward himself two of the officers fired their tasers, both shots landing in his chest. Marcus thought it was the most peculiar sensation. It felt like a mega-sized joy buzzer had gone off in his mid-section. It was the kind of pain that made him grunt in an effort to release the feeling through his mouth. He dropped to the ground and Craig tried to fight the electricity, but the other two officers were on him, telling him to stay down and hold still.

Craig receded and Marcus took control. He felt the vague buzzing sensation that remained, but the pain from the officers wrenching his arms behind him and cuffing him outweighed the sensation. Vaguely, Marcus wondered if he hadn't felt the full effect, because Craig had been the one in charge in that moment. He thought he was quite grateful for that little mercy if that were the case. A little shock therapy for the villain.

Out of the corner of his eye he saw the lead officer asking if John and his children were okay, and he saw them nodding and hugging each other. Marcus decided to recede with the others in his head and let nature take its course. He had some things to settle with his new roommates.

Craig was sitting in a far corner, looking a little crispy, which brought a smile to Marcus's face. "Back at you," Craig said, raising a middle finger to Marcus.

Maria sat on the ground, breathing heavily. She looked absolutely exhausted. He walked over to her and sat beside her. "It's over now. Let the rest of it begin. We got him and there is nothing he can do about it. At least from here on we will get three squares and feel good drugs."

Maria leaned against him and let out a sigh. "Yep. We got him. Might as well enjoy our victory."

Maria and Marcus laughed and looked over at Craig who eyeballed them sourly. Marcus conjured a cap onto his head and doffed it at Craig. "Thank you kindly for your part in this multi-act play. You played your character brilliantly." Craig turned away, a string of expletives flowing over his lips, and Marcus smiled.

He fell asleep in the back of the police cruiser, allowing himself to finally relax. It was all as good as it would be, and he could rest in that knowledge.

EPILOGUE

Marcus walked down the white hall in his white jumper, wrist and ankle bracelets clattering along as he went. He had been in the medium security hospital for about three months and was getting used to the routine. When he was sedated, Craig could come forward, but he wasn't able to take full control. And when Craig did attempt to take over he would mouth off to the guards, which earned him an electric treatment or a needle in the rear with a cocktail that calmed him right down. Craig was trying less and less as time went on, but Marcus had a feeling he was simply biding his time, which was fine with Marcus, because the sentencing had put him in the hospital for ten years. Marcus planned on making it through most of the sentence and then allowing Craig to take control just long enough to extend their visit.

The only problem was the plan was contingent on Craig remaining angry enough to not see the plan or figure it out. And Craig was plenty angry. Not a day went by where he didn't have some sort of outburst. Most of the time they came when the three of them were alone in their room, so that was okay. He also talked nearly non-stop, which *did* drive the other two a little crazy, but, hey, they were at this hospital for a reason. Maria didn't know of Marcus's plan to keep them incarcerated for an extended period of time, but he had a feeling she would approve.

As for Maria, she was content and would often leave to go to her Garden Room when they were drugged. She figured that was the only really safe time to leave Craig semi-unattended. Marcus and Maria shared a fear that if Craig were to gain enough control he would be able to retain that control for good; that he might be able to crack Marcus's sanity in such a way as to send him drifting off into his own mind permanently. That idea did not appeal to Marcus.

Sometimes Craig would go to his sick dungeon and Maria used those opportunities to head to her Garden Room as well. She enjoyed being fully cognitive in her happy place when she was able. And Marcus fully enjoyed the solitude, even if it was short-lived.

Marcus had even figured out a way to rig a bell system to recall Maria when Craig returned from his place.

Maria also got a visit once a week from her husband, and once a month from her kids, which is where they were headed now. It was just a husband visit, so it wouldn't be as long and drawn out. Marcus knew he would have to endure the judging looks from John, but he was able to hang out in his head for the most part.

On occasion, John would want to talk to Craig, but more often than not he was content with speaking to Maria and leaving it at that. Mostly Craig remained civil with his brother, but then he would lash out, berating his brother for not being stronger, using every colorful word and phrase at his disposal to get his point across, and John would leave looking like a wounded pet. The only nice part of the tongue lashings John got from Craig was watching Maria turn on Craig after the encounters. She had her own version of vibrant language that, if Marcus was being honest, put Craig's pedestrian uses to shame. Maybe he was biased, but he thought not.

Marcus *was* grateful that none of the visits were conjugal. He figured that would have been a little too weird, since the physical body was still that of Marcus's, but he always saw that little spark in John's eyes when Maria was talking to him. They talked about so many things and Marcus gave them as much privacy as he was able, and whenever Marcus tried to say anything to John the conversation would abruptly end. John refused to talk to him; still blamed him for the state his wife was in, even though it had been her idea. But Marcus didn't mind; he was actually quite content with his living situation. He kept mostly to himself and occasionally played chess or checkers with one of the other patients, because that's what they were called in this facility, patients. He tried to ignore Craig when he could and enjoyed long conversations with Maria.

They finally made it to the visiting room and saw John sitting at the table and Maria immediately took control. Marcus headed off into his own mind, ignoring the lewd gestures Craig was making, trying to find a place apart from him.

As Marcus wandered inside his own head, he mused at the inane question that interviewers always liked to ask prospective employees: Where do you see yourself in five years? Well, if an interviewer had asked Marcus that question a little over three months ago, he wouldn't have known how to answer, and he would have scoffed if that interviewer told him his entire life was about to change forever. But now he could answer that question easily. He could look the interviewer directly in the eyes and say with confidence, "I will be right where I'm supposed to be. It may not be where I intended when I first started on the journey, but it is where I am needed. And that is good enough for me." And the interviewer would stand up and shake Marcus's hand and let him know that they would be in touch and

Marcus would know exactly what that meant, and he would turn on his brightest smile and reply, "Thank you and a nice day to you too."

ACKNOWLEDGEMENTS

This has been a labor of existential terror and deep love for inherent goodness of humanity. I have children and living in this world can be terrifying at times. Writing this book allowed me to separate my anxiety from reality and the people around me have helped with that as well.

To my parents: Thank you for always encouraging me to explore my dreams and reach out into the unknown and pull out of it something new.

To my test readers: You all helped me hone my story and find some egregious continuity errors that would have knocked the story completely flat. And you helped me elaborate on pieces of the story that were unclear. They mystery is alive and well in this story because of you.

To my wife: You are my partner, my love, my inspiration to pursue my dreams, and you always have confidence in me, even when I fail to see it myself.

THE WOOD WILL SWALLOW YOU WHOLE

COMING SOON

TURN THE PAGE FOR A SHORT STORY FROM
THIS COLLECTION

ALL THE LAND YOU OWN

You own a plot of land. On this plot of land there is a pond. In this pond lives a school of fish, a whole host of frogs, and an underwater treasure. A Great heron visits the pond once a day to scoop up one of the fish, yet the number never dwindles.

One day, as you walk your land you notice a tear in the ground. It isn't that some machine has come through and tilled up the soil. It's more of a gaping wound that has not been sewn back together with sutures. This tear makes you sad. It reminds you that life is fragile and even the earth beneath your feet is not immune to the violence of existence.

You follow the tear and discover that it leads directly to the pond. The gouge is below the water line, yet none of the water splashes over onto this ground. It's as if someone has placed a sheet of glass between the water and the dirt to hold it in place.

Curiosity takes hold and you return to your house to find a pickaxe and shovel. But as you walk you find yourself getting turned around. The common path you are used to walking every day becomes muddled in your head. It's like someone is rearranging thoughts in your brain to purposefully confuse you.

You stop.

You take a deep breath.

You allow your thoughts to coalesce into remembrance and then you continue your journey.

As you wander you see all the land you have tilled and dug into. The pieces of land you avoid because they remind you of something horrible and destructive. A shiver convulses your body, and your mouth runs dry.

How long have you been walking?

You don't ever recall it taking this long to walk from the pond to your house before.

In the distance you see the structure you are striving for, and a sense of relief falls over you. It isn't until this moment you realize your heart is beating too fast in your chest.

Although the house is within your eyesight you sit to take a rest.

You listen to the sounds of nature.

It is soothing.

You recall fishing in a lake when you were a child; your father next to you; a million gnats buzzing around your head.

But now you have aged, and you can feel the cold settle into your bones and aches come and go without so much as an invitation.

You can't recall what you were going to the house for, but hunger hits you like a brick wall. If you don't eat something soon you know you will feel faint and perhaps even pass out as your blood sugar plummets. So, you pick yourself up off the ground and continue your journey to the house.

A patch of unfamiliar ground rises in front of you, and you furrow your brow trying to remember the last time you came this way on your land.

You question if you've ever approached the house from this particular angle before, but you cannot recall.

At least you can see the house from here, so you can reach your destination.

Finally, after what feels like ages, your hand touches the familiar chill of the knob attached to the front door. You step inside, but immediately sense something is wrong. Although you cannot recall how long you have lived on this land by yourself, you know it has been quite some time.

There are picture frames lining the walls of the entryway, smiling faces you seem to know watching you walk toward the kitchen. They are vaguely familiar, but the names elude you.

Now that you are in the house you have lost track of the task you originally intended to accomplish. Instead of worrying about it, you decide to make yourself a sandwich, but when you search for a butter knife you discover that everything has been rearranged in the drawers, which makes no sense, since you live here alone, and no one ever comes to visit.

The anger takes hold and you fling drawers open, throwing them to the ground, watching utensils and pens and rubber bands and papers crash to the floor in a tumult of sound that makes you cover your ears in self-preservation.

You throw open the fridge and stand in front of the artificial light, wolfing down lunch meat and cheese until the dryness in your throat demands resolution as the choking feeling almost overwhelms you. And you rummage through the cabinets but are unable to find a single glass to fill.

The rage builds inside once again as you wonder exactly who in hell could have moved your items around.

As the fury subsides, you walk to the sink, dip your head under the running faucet, and drink deeply until your throat is no longer scratchy.

This act reminds you of your original intent with coming up to the house and you grab a pickaxe and a shovel and head back outside.

Upon your return to the pond, you notice that the tear has deepened, and yet still none of the water has leaked into the culvert. You imagine that if you could somehow allow the water to pass through to the dry earth all will be all right.

You put your hand against the invisible barrier between water and dirt and feel the pressure there.

It is almost unbearable.

So, you begin to work the ground, creating more space for the water to rush to, but no matter how much room you create, the water holds its shape and refuses to spill over and dampen the earth.

As you investigate this strange anomaly you notice a small wooden box nestled in a tangle of underwater weeds and rocks.

It looks old and warped.

Worn away from years of neglect.

You remove your shoes and socks and roll up your pant legs and wade into the pond. Fish scurry away, leaving bubble trails in their wake. Frogs hope from rock to rock, croaking in disapproval at the disturbance.

The water gets deeper and deeper until you realize your chest is under the surface. You feel around with your toes until they graze the top of the box.

Without hesitation you dive, looking for the exact spot your foot landed on moments before.

There is no air in your lungs. It feels as though you have forgotten the mechanics of breathing while simultaneously understanding that if you were to achieve the breath you so desperately need you would drown.

But the box persists.

As do you.

Panic begins to overcome you, but still, you struggle with the box.

Then your finger finds a latch and you open the box, needing to see what treasure lies within, even if it takes your last breath. And as the lid opens on its hinges you hear a melody. Something you haven't heard in years, possibly decades.

Pictures float out of the box, and you grab onto them as they pass by, floating to the surface.

And you know the faces in the photos.

They beckon for you to follow them to the surface, and you obey.

The sensation of flowing water tugs at your clothing, and you realize that the invisible dam has burst open, and the pond is expanding to heal the tear.

As you emerge from the water you realize you do in fact remember how to breathe and you inhale a lung full of air, grasping the photos tight in your fist.

And the melody persists, reminding you of everything you have ever forgotten.

Your house swims into focus and you recall where everything should be, and is, and you begin to cry.

Clarity rushes in and you hold tight to the memories.

An impending sense of déjà vu overwhelms you and as you trudge back to your home you pray that if you are cursed to repeat the same day over again, that you remember how to breathe.